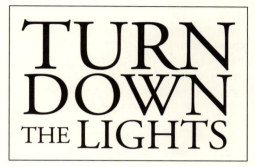

Edited by
RICHARD CHIZMAR

CEMETERY DANCE PUBLICATIONS

*Baltimore*
❖ 2013 ❖

Copyright © 2013 by Richard Chizmar

Individual stories Copyright © 2013 by their respective authors.

All rights reserved. No part of this book may be reproduced in any form or by any electronic or mechanical means, including information storage and retrieval systems, without permission in writing from the publisher, except by a reviewer who may quote brief passages in a review.

Cemetery Dance Publications
132-B Industry Lane, Unit #7
Forest Hill, MD 21050
http://www.cemeterydance.com

The characters and events in this book are fictitious. Any similarity to real persons, living or dead, is coincidental and not intended by the authors.

First Trade Hardcover Printing

ISBN-13: 978-1-58767-437-2

Cover Artwork Copyright © 2013 by Alan M. Clark
Cover Artwork for *Cemetery Dance #1* Copyright © 1988 by Bill Caughron
Cover Design by Desert Isle Design
Interior Design by Kate Freeman Design

*For Billy and Noah,
my two favorite stories...*

# TABLE OF CONTENTS

Turn Down the Lights…     9
*Richard Chizmar*

Summer Thunder     17
*Stephen King*

Incarnadine     39
*Norman Partridge*

The Western Dead     51
*Jack Ketchum*

An Instant Eternity     63
*Brian James Freeman*

In the Room     87
*Bentley Little*

Flying Solo     101
*Ed Gorman*

The Outhouse     127
*Ronald Kelly*

Lookie-Loo     139
*Steve Rasnic Tem*

Dollie     149
*Clive Barker*

The Collected Stories of Freddie Prothero     157
Introduction by Torless Magnussen, Ph.D.
*Peter Straub*

Afterword     169
*Thomas F. Monteleone*

# Richard Chizmar

It was December 1988: George Bush had just defeated Michael Dukakis in the Presidential Election. Pitcher Orel Hershiser and the Los Angeles Dodgers had beaten the Oakland A's in five games to win the World Series. People were waiting in line at movie theaters to watch Tom Cruise and Dustin Hoffman in *Rain Man*. Tom Clancy's *The Cardinal of the Kremlin* and Anne Rice's *The Queen of the Damned* were atop the bestseller lists. The most acclaimed genre books of the year were Thomas Harris's *The Silence of the Lambs* and Peter Straub's *Koko*.

I was 22 years old. And I decided to publish a magazine named *Cemetery Dance*.

# RICHARD CHIZMAR

At the time, I was studying journalism at the University of Maryland and selling short stories of a dark nature to any publication that would accept them. Some of these publications were professional and impressive. Many others, not so much. So—inspired by the brilliance of David Silva's one-man magazine *The Horror Show*—I asked myself the question that has been responsible for most all of my crazier ideas: *why not?*

Why not dive right in and publish a magazine that showcased both seasoned pros and talented newcomers?

Why not publish the type of genre-blurring dark fiction I preferred to read and write myself: horror, suspense, crime.

Why not publish fiction alongside interviews and book reviews and genre commentary?

Why not open up to story submissions during summer break and schedule the premiere issue six months later in December?

Why not try to create something truly special?

The idea that I had no experience, no money, no business plan never really entered into the equation.

Dreams are for the courageous and the foolish. Cowards need not apply.

*Why the hell not?*

Did I mention I was 22 years old?

—⚞—

The premiere issue of *Cemetery Dance* was only 48 pages in length. It contained a dozen short stories, a dozen poems, an interview with David Silva, and cover and

# TURN DOWN THE LIGHTS...

interior artwork by Bill Caughron. I should mention that Bill was my college roommate and childhood friend and the only guy I knew at the time who could draw. I can still remember him drawing interior spot illustrations right on the laser-printed pages of designed text. He drew the front cover sitting at our dining room table while I hurled darts over his head at a dartboard, nervously checking his progress every few minutes. I can also remember Bill and I hitting the PRINT button in the University of Maryland computer lab and running out of the room. You see, there was a very large sign posted above the printer that clearly stated: *do not print more than 10 pages at a time.* Laser printers were fairly slow back in those days, so suffice to say we were not very popular with the other students when we returned an hour later to collect our 96 pages. That's right; we printed two copies. We were no dummies.

That first issue may have only run 48 pages, but it represented thousands of hours of work. Writing and mailing query letters. Making phone calls. Reading stories. Rejecting stories. Begging for stories. Trying to sell advertisements. Paying for advertisements in other publications to try to raise funds for printing. Designing interior pages. There was no guidebook. No roadmap except what existed inside my head. Almost everything came from instinct and imagination and passion. And making and learning from mistakes along the way.

Thankfully, I had Dave Silva to help me avoid some of those mistakes; he answered questions at all times of the day and night; he was a friend and a mentor. Encouraging me. Believing in me.

Still…for every success, there seemed to be a failure. Sometimes two or three. But I rarely felt discouraged or had doubts. I was having the time of my young life, and I sensed there was…*something* here. Maybe something special. I just had to keep working at it. I just had to keep believing.

The first issue was released right on time in December, and I remember we already had most of the second issue in the can. And R.C. Matheson lined up to feature in the third issue.

It was never a question of whether we would continue.

It was never a question of success or failure.

From the very beginning, it just *was*.

Why not, right?

—⁂—

When I realized that we were coming up on 25 years since that premiere issue was published I knew I wanted to do…*something*.

Something personal to mark the anniversary and the long journey we had all made together.

So much had happened in those 25 years: the magazine had spawned a hardcover book imprint…and trade paperbacks…and comics…and t-shirts…and electronic books…and cool things still to come.

And so much had happened in real life, too: marriage, two amazing children, the loss of my oldest sister, cancer, cancer again a year later, the loss of my parents.

# TURN DOWN THE LIGHTS...

In other words...*life* happened.

And, somehow, Cemetery Dance was there to witness all of it.

To be a part of all of it.

---

The book you hold in your hands is very personal to me.

In a way, it's my own little celebration party 25 years later.

There is a reason it's a small book. I wanted to include only the handful of writers who, in my mind, were as responsible for Cemetery Dance existing today as I am myself.

I won't go into each individual writer. They know why they are here.

A few authors couldn't make it because of their schedules—I only decided to put this together two weeks ago; why not, right?—although they each said they wanted to.

And, sadly, still another handful are missing. I wish Dave Silva were alive to appear in these pages. The same goes for Charlie Grant and Rick Hautala and Bill Relling. They all believed in me during those early days, and their faith meant so much.

---

It's December 2013: I owe such a debt of gratitude to each and every person who ever lent their talents to

# RICHARD CHIZMAR

the magazine; to an amazing full-time staff and a slew of part-timers; and to the wonderful readers who kept asking for more. I have no way to repay you other than to continue doing what I have been doing these past 25 years. I hope it's enough.

Now, turn down the lights, flip the page, take my hand, and start the dance...

Richard Chizmar
October 23, 2013

# CEMETERY DANCE

**PREMIERE ISSUE**

David B. Silva Special

December 1988

$3.95

# SUMMER THUNDER

*Stephen King*

Robinson was okay as long as Gandalf was. Not okay in the sense of everything is fine, but in the sense of getting along from day to day. He still woke up in the night, often with tears on his face from dreams—so vivid!—where Diana and Ellen were alive, but when he picked Gandalf up from the blankets in the corner where he slept and put him on the bed, he could more often than not go back to sleep again. As for Gandalf, he didn't care where he slept, and if Robinson pulled him close, that was okay, too. It was warm, dry, and safe. He had been rescued. That was all Gandalf cared about.

With another living being to take care of, things were better. Robinson drove to the country store five miles up Route 19 (Gandalf sitting in the pickup's passenger seat, ears cocked, eyes bright) and got dog food. The store was abandoned, and of course it had been looted, but no one had taken the Eukanuba. After June Sixth, pets had been about the last thing on people's minds. So Robinson deduced.

Otherwise, the two of them stayed by the lake. There was plenty of food in the pantry, and boxes of stuff downstairs. He had often joked about how Diana expected the apocalypse, but the joke turned out to be on him. Both of them, really, because Diana had surely never imagined that when the apocalypse came, she would be in Boston with their daughter, investigating the academic possibilities of Emerson College. Eating for one, the food would last longer than he did. Robinson had no doubt of that. Timlin said they were doomed.

If so, doom was beautiful. The weather was warm and cloudless. In the old days, Lake Pocomtuc would have buzzed with powerboats and jet-skis (which were killing the fish, the oldtimers grumbled), but this summer it was silent except for the loons…only there seemed to be fewer of them crying each night. At first Robinson thought this was just his imagination, which was as infected with grief as the rest of his thinking apparatus, but Timlin assured him it wasn't.

"Haven't you noticed that most of the woodland birds are already gone? No chickadee concerts in the morning, no crow-music at noon. By September, the loons will be as gone as the loons who did this. The fish will live a little longer, but eventually they'll be gone, too. Like the deer, the rabbits, and the chipmunks."

About such wildlife there could be no argument. Robinson had seen almost a dozen dead deer beside the lake road and more beside Route 19 on that one trip he and Gandalf had made to the Carson Corners General

# SUMMER THUNDER

Store, where the sign out front—BUY YOUR VERMONT CHEESE & SYRUP HERE!—now lay facedown next to the dry gas pumps. But the greatest part of the animal holocaust was in the woods. When the wind was from the east, toward the lake rather than off it, the reek was tremendous. The warm days didn't help, and Robinson wanted to know what had happened to nuclear winter.

"Oh, it'll come," said Timlin, sitting in his rocker and looking off into the dappled sunshine under the trees. "Earth is still absorbing the blow. Besides, we know from the last reports that the southern hemisphere—not to mention most of Asia—is socked in beneath what may turn out to be eternal cloud cover. Enjoy the sunshine while we've got it, Peter."

As if he could enjoy anything. He and Diana had been talking about a trip to England—their first extended vacation since the honeymoon—once Ellen was settled in school.

Ellen, he thought. Who had just been recovering from the break-up with her first real boyfriend and was beginning to smile again.

—⚭—

On each of these fine late summer post-apocalypse days, Robinson clipped a leash to Gandalf's collar (he had no idea what the dog's name had been before June Sixth; the mutt had come with a collar from which only a State of Massachusetts vaccination tag hung), and they walked the two miles to the pricey enclave of which Howard Timlin was now the only resident.

Diana had once called that walk snapshot heaven. Much of it overlooked sheer drops to the lake and forty-mile views into New York. At one point, where the road buttonhooked sharply, a sign that read MIND YOUR DRIVING! had been posted. The summer kids of course called this hairpin Dead Man's Curve.

Woodland Acres—private as well as pricey before the world ended—was a mile further on. The centerpiece was a fieldstone lodge that had featured a restaurant with a marvelous view, a five-star chef, and a "beer pantry" stocked with a thousand brands. ("Many of them undrinkable," Timlin said. "Take it from me.") Scattered around the main lodge, in various bosky dells, were two dozen picturesque "cottages," some owned by major corporations before June Sixth put an end to corporations. Most of the cottages had still been empty on June Sixth, and in the crazy days that followed, the few people who were in residence fled for Canada, which was rumored to be radiation-free. That was when there was still gasoline to make flight possible.

The owners of Woodland Acres, George and Ellen Benson, had stayed. So had Timlin, who was divorced, had no children to mourn, and knew the Canada story was surely a fable. Then, in early July, the Bensons had swallowed pills and taken to their bed while listening to Beethoven on a battery-powered phonograph. Now it was just Timlin.

"All that you see is mine," he had told Robinson, waving his arm grandly. "And someday, son, it will be yours."

On these daily walks down to the Acres, Robinson's grief and sense of dislocation eased a bit; sunshine was

# SUMMER THUNDER

seductive. Gandalf sniffed at the bushes and tried to pee on every one. He barked bravely when he heard something in the woods, but always moved closer to Robinson. The leash was necessary only because of the dead squirrels and chipmunks. Gandalf didn't want to pee on those; he wanted to roll in what was left of them.

Woodland Acres Lane split off from the camp road where Robinson now lived the single life. Once the lane had been gated to keep lookie-loos and wage-slave rabble such as himself out, but now the gate stood permanently open. The lane meandered for half a mile through forest where the slanting, dusty light seemed almost as old as the towering spruces and pines that filtered it, passed four tennis courts, skirted a putting green, and looped behind a barn where the trail horses now lay dead in their stalls. Timlin's cottage was on the far side of the lodge—a modest dwelling with four bedrooms, four bathrooms, a hot tub, and its own sauna.

"Why did you need four bedrooms, if it's just you?" Robinson asked him once.

"I don't now and never did," Timlin said, "but they *all* have four bedrooms. Except for Foxglove, Yarrow, and Lavender. They have five. Lavender also has an attached bowling alley. All mod cons. But when I came here as a kid with my family, we peed in a privy. True thing."

Robinson and Gandalf usually found Timlin sitting in one of the rockers on the wide front porch of his cottage (Veronica), reading a book or listening to his iPod. Robinson would unclip the leash from Gandalf's collar and the dog—just a mutt, no real recognizable breed except for the spaniel ears—raced up the steps to be made of. After a few strokes, Timlin would gently pull at the dog's gray-white fur in various places, and when it remained rooted, he would always say the same thing: "Remarkable."

—⚍—

On this fine day in mid-August, Gandalf only made a brief visit to Timlin's rocker, sniffing at the man's bare ankles before trotting back down the steps and into the woods. Timlin raised his hand to Robinson in the How gesture of an old-time movie Indian. Robinson returned the compliment.

"Want a beer?" Timlin asked. "They're cool. I just dragged them out of the lake."

"Would today's tipple be Old Shitty or Green Mountain Dew?"

"Neither. There was a case of Budweiser in the storeroom. The King of Beers, as you may remember. I liberated it."

"In that case, I'll be happy to join you."

Timlin got up with a grunt and went inside, rocking slightly from side to side. Arthritis had mounted a sneak attack on his hips, he had told Robinson, and, not content with that, had decided to lay claim to his ankles. Robinson had never asked, but judged Timlin to be in his mid-seventies. His slim body suggested a life of fitness, but fitness was now beginning to fail. Robinson himself had never felt physically better in his life, which was ironic considering how little he now had to live for. Timlin certainly didn't need him, although he was congenial enough. As this preternaturally beautiful summer wound down, only Gandalf actually needed him. Which was okay, because for now, Gandalf was enough.

Just a boy and his dog, he thought.

Said dog had emerged from the woods in mid-June, thin and bedraggled, his coat snarled with burdocks and with a deep scratch across his snout. Robinson had been lying in the guest bedroom (he could not bear to sleep in the bed he had shared with Diana), sleepless with grief and depression, aware that he was edging closer and closer to just giving up and pulling the pin. He would have called such an action cowardly only weeks before, but had since come to recognize several undeniable facts. The pain would not stop. The grief would not stop. And, of course, his life was not apt to be a long one in any case. You only had to smell the decaying animals in the woods to know that.

He'd heard rattling sounds, and at first thought it might be a human being. Or a bear that had smelled his food. But the gennie was still running then, and the motion lights that illuminated the driveway had come on, and when he looked out the window he saw a little gray dog, alternately scratching at the door and then huddling on the porch. When Robinson opened the door, the dog at first backed away, ears back and tail tucked.

"You better come in," Robinson had said. "If you can't follow your nose, just follow the goddam mosquitoes."

He gave the dog a bowl of water, which he lapped furiously, and then a can of Prudence corned beef hash, which he ate in five or six huge bites. When the dog finished, Robinson stroked him, hoping he wouldn't be bitten. Instead of biting, the dog licked his hand.

"You're Gandalf," Robinson had said. "Gandalf the Grey." And then burst into tears. He tried to tell himself he was being ridiculous, but he wasn't. The dog was, after all, a living being. He was no longer alone in the house.

---

"What is the news about that motorcycle of yours?" Timlin asked.

They had progressed to their second beers. When Robinson finished his, he and Gandalf would make the two-mile trek back to the house. He didn't want to wait too long; the mosquitoes got thicker when twilight came.

*If Timlin's right,* he thought, *the bloodsuckers will inherit the earth instead of the meek. If they can find any blood to suck, that is.*

"The battery's dead," he told Timlin. Then: "My wife made me promise to sell the bike when I was fifty. She said after fifty, a man's reflexes are too slow to be safe."

"And you're fifty when?"

"Next year," Robinson said. And laughed at the absurdity of it.

"I lost a tooth this morning," Timlin said. "Might mean nothing at my age, but…"

"Seeing any blood in the toilet bowl?"

Timlin—a professor emeritus who had, until last year, still taught an American history seminar at Princeton—had told him that was one of the first signs of advanced radiation poisoning, and he knew a lot more about it than Robinson did. What Robinson knew was that his wife and daughter had been in Boston when the frantic Geneva

# SUMMER THUNDER

peace talks had gone up in a nuclear flash on the fifth of June, and they were still in Boston the next day, when the world killed itself. The eastern seaboard, from Hartford to Miami, was now mostly slag.

"I'm going to take the Fifth on that," Timlin said. "Here comes your dog. Better check his paws—he's limping a bit. Looks like the rear left."

But they could find no thorn in any of Gandalf's paws, and this time when Timlin pulled gently at his fur, a patch on his hindquarters came out. Gandalf seemed not to feel it.

"Not good," Timlin said.

"Could be the mange," Robinson said. "Or stress. Dogs do lose fur when they're stressed, you know."

"Maybe." Timlin was looking west, across the lake. "It's going to be a beautiful sunset. Of course, they're all beautiful now. Like when Krakatoa blew its stack in 1883. Only this was ten thousand Krakatoas." He bent and stroked Gandalf's head.

"India and Pakistan," Robinson said.

Timlin straightened up again. "Well, yes. But then everyone else just had to get into the act, didn't they? Even the Chechens had a few, which they delivered to Moscow in pickup trucks. It's as though the world willfully forgot how many countries—and groups, fucking *groups!*—had those things."

"Or what those things were capable of," Robinson said.

Timlin nodded. "That, too. We were too worried about the debt ceiling, and our friends across the pond were concentrating on stopping child beauty pageants and propping up the euro."

"You're sure Canada's just as dirty as the lower forty-eight?"

"It's a matter of degree, I suppose. Vermont's not as dirty as upstate New York, and Canada's probably not as dirty as Vermont. But it will be. Plus, most of the people headed up there are already sick. Sick unto death, if I may misquote Kierkegaard. Want another beer?"

"I'd better get back." Robinson stood. "Come on, Gandalf. Time to burn some calories."

"Will I see you tomorrow?"

"Maybe in the late afternoon. I've got an errand to run in the morning."

"May I ask where?"

"Bennington, while there's still enough gas in my truck to get there and back."

Timlin raised his eyebrows.

"Want to see if I can find a motorcycle battery."

—⚝—

Gandalf made it as far as Dead Man's Curve under his own power, although his limp grew steadily worse. When they got there, he simply sat down, as if to watch the boiling sunset reflected in the lake. It was a fuming orange shot through with arteries of deepest red. The dog whined and licked at his back left leg. Robinson sat beside him for a little while, but when the first mosquito scouts called for reinforcements, he picked Gandalf up and started walking again. By the time they got back to the house, Robinson's arms were trembling and his shoulders were aching. If Gandalf had weighed another ten pounds, maybe even another five, he doubted if he could have made it. His head also ached, perhaps from the heat, or the second beer, or both.

The tree-lined driveway sloping down to the house was a pool of shadows, and the house itself was dark. The gennie had given up the ghost weeks ago. Sunset had subsided to a dull purple bruise. He plodded onto the porch and put Gandalf down to open the door. "Go on, boy," he said. Gandalf struggled to rise, then subsided.

Just as Robinson was bending to pick him up again, Gandalf made another effort. This time he got over the doorsill and into the entryway, where he collapsed on his side, panting. On the wall above him were at least two dozen photographs featuring the people Robinson loved, all of them now presumably deceased. He could no longer even dial Diana and Ellen's phones and listen to their recorded voices. His own phone had died shortly after the generator, but even before that, all cell service had ceased.

He got a bottle of Poland Spring water from the pantry, filled Gandalf's bowl, then put down a scoop of kibble. Gandalf drank some water but wouldn't eat. When Robinson squatted to scratch the dog's belly, fur came out in bundles.

It's happening so fast, he thought. This morning he was fine.

—⁂—

He took a flashlight and went out to the lean-to behind the house. On the lake, a loon cried—just one. The motorcycle was under a tarp. He pulled the canvas off and shone the beam along the bike's gleaming body. It was a 2014 Fat Bob, several years old now, but low mileage; his days of riding four and five thousand miles between May and October were behind him. Yet the Bob was still his dream ride, even though his dreams were mostly where he'd ridden it over the last couple of years. Air-cooled. Twin cam. Six-speed. Almost seventeen hundred ccs. And the sound it made! Only Harleys had that sound, like summer thunder. When you came up next to a Chevy at a stoplight, the cager inside was apt to lock his doors.

Robinson skidded a palm along the handlebars, then hoisted his leg over and sat in the saddle with his feet on the pegs. Diana had become increasingly insistent that he sell it, and when he did ride, she reminded him again and again that Vermont had a helmet law for a reason… unlike the idiots in New Hampshire and Maine. Now he could ride it without a helmet if he wanted to. There was no Diana to nag him, and no County Mounties to pull him over. He could ride it buckass naked, if he wanted to.

"Although I'd have to mind the tailpipes when I got off," he said, and laughed. He went inside without putting the tarp back on the Harley. Gandalf was lying on the bed of blankets Robinson had made for him, nose on one of his front paws. His kibble was untouched.

"Better eat up," Robinson said. "You'll feel better."

—⚋—

The next morning there was a red stain on the blankets around Gandalf's hindquarters, and although he tried, he couldn't quite make it to his feet. After he

# SUMMER THUNDER

gave up the second time, Robinson carried him outside, where Gandalf first lay on the grass, then managed to get up enough to squat. What came out of him was a gush of bloody stool. Gandalf crawled away from it as if ashamed, then lay down, looking at Robinson mournfully.

This time when Robinson picked him up, Gandalf cried out in pain and bared his teeth but did not bite. Robinson carried him into the house and put him down on his blanket bed. He looked at his hands when he straightened up and saw they were coated with fur. When he dusted his palms together, it floated down like milkweed.

"You'll be okay," he told Gandalf. "Just a little upset stomach. Must have gotten one of those goddam chipmunks when I wasn't looking. Stay there and rest up. I'm sure you'll be feeling more yourself by the time I get back."

—◊—

There was still half a tank of gas in the Silverado, more than enough for the sixty-mile round trip to Bennington. Robinson decided to go down to Woodland Acres first and see if Timlin wanted anything.

His last neighbor was sitting on the porch of Veronica in his rocker. He was pale, and there were purple pouches under his eyes. When Robinson told him about Gandalf, Timlin nodded. "I was up most of the night, running to the toilet. We must have caught the same bug." He smiled to show it was a joke…although not a very funny one.

No, he said, there was nothing he wanted in Bennington, but perhaps Robinson would stop by on his way back. "I've got something *you* might want," he said.

# STEPHEN KING

—⚡—

The drive to Bennington was slower than Robinson expected, because the highway was littered with abandoned cars. It was close to noon by the time he pulled into the front lot of Kingdom Harley-Davidson. The show windows had been broken and all the display models were gone, but there were plenty of bikes out back. These had been rendered theft-proof with steel cables and sturdy bike-locks.

That was fine with Robinson; he only wanted a battery. The Fat Bob he settled on was a year or two newer than his, but the battery looked the same. He fetched his toolbox from the bed of his pickup and checked the battery with his Impact (the tester had been a gift from his daughter two birthdays back), and got a green light. He removed the battery, went into the showroom, and found a selection of maps. Using the most detailed one to suss out the secondary roads, he made it back to the lake by three o'clock.

He saw a great many dead animals, including an extremely large moose lying beside the cement block steps of someone's trailer home. On the trailer's crabgrassy lawn, a hand-painted sign had been posted, only two words: HEAVEN SOON.

—⚡—

The porch of Veronica was deserted, but when Robinson knocked on the door, Timlin called for him to come in. He was sitting in the ostentatiously rustic living room, paler than ever. In one hand he held an oversized linen napkin. It was spotted with blood. On the coffee table in front of him were three items: an oversized book titled *The Beauty of Vermont*, a hypodermic needle filled with yellow fluid, and a revolver.

"I'm glad you came," Timlin said. "I didn't want to leave without telling you goodbye."

Robinson recognized the absurdity of the first response that came to mind—*Let's not be hasty*—and managed to stay silent.

"I've lost half a dozen teeth," Timlin said, "but that's not the major development. In the last twelve hours or so, I seem to have expelled most of my intestines. The eerie thing is how little it hurts. The hemorrhoids I was afflicted with in my fifties were worse. The pain will come—I've read enough to know that—but I don't intend to stick around long enough to experience it in full flower. Did you get the battery you wanted?"

"Yes," Robinson said, and sat down heavily. "Jesus, Howard, I'm sorry."

"And you? How do you feel?"

"Fine." Although this was no longer completely true. Several red patches that didn't look like sunburn were blooming on his forearms, and there was another on his chest, above the right nipple. They itched. Also…his breakfast was staying down, but his stomach seemed far from happy with it.

Timlin leaned forward and tapped the hypo. "Demerol. I was going to inject myself, then look at pictures of Vermont until…until. But I've changed my mind. The gun will be fine, I think. You take the hypo."

"I'm not quite ready," Robinson said.

"It's not for you. Gandalf doesn't deserve to suffer."

"I think maybe he just ate a chipmunk," Robinson said feebly.

"We both know that's not it. Even if it was, the dead animals are so full of radiation it might as well have been a cobalt capsule. It's a wonder he's survived as long as he has. Be grateful for the time you've had with him. A little bit of grace. That's what a good dog is, you know. A little bit of grace."

Timlin studied him closely.

"Don't you cry on me. If you do, I will too, so man the fuck up."

Robinson managed not to cry, although he did not in truth feel very manly.

"There's one more sixpack of Bud in the fridge," Timlin said. "I don't know why I bothered to put it in there, but old habits die hard. Why don't you bring us each one? Warm beer is better than no beer; I believe Woodrow Wilson said that. We'll toast Gandalf. Also your new motorcycle battery. Meanwhile, I need to spend a penny. Or, who knows, this one might cost a little more."

Robinson got the beer. When he came back Timlin was gone, and remained gone for almost five minutes. He came back slowly, holding onto things. He had removed his pants and cinched a bath sheet around his midsection. He sat down with a little cry of pain, but took the can of beer Robinson held out to him. They toasted Gandalf and drank. The Bud was warm, all right, but not that bad. It was, after all, the King of Beers.

## SUMMER THUNDER

Timlin picked up the gun. "Mine will be the classic Victorian suicide," he said, sounding pleased at the prospect. "Gun to temple. Free hand over the eyes. Goodbye, cruel world."

"I'm off to join the circus," Robinson said without thinking.

Timlin laughed heartily, lips peeling back to reveal his few remaining teeth. "It would be nice, but I doubt it. Did I ever tell you that I was hit by a truck when I was a boy? The kind our British cousins call a milk float?"

Robinson shook his head.

"1957, this was. I was fifteen, walking down a country road in Michigan, headed for Highway 22, where I hoped to hook a ride into Traverse City and attend a double-feature movieshow. I was daydreaming about a girl in my homeroom—such long, lovely legs and such high breasts—and wandered away from the relative safety of the shoulder. The milk float came over the top of a hill—the driver was going much too fast—and hit me square on. If it had been fully loaded, I surely would have been killed, but because it was empty it was much lighter, allowing me to live to the age of seventy-five, and experience what it's like to shit one's bowels into a toilet that will no longer flush."

There seemed to be no adequate response to this, so Robinson kept quiet.

"There was a flash of sun on the float's windshield as it came over the top of the hill, and then...nothing. I believe I will experience roughly the same thing when the bullet goes into my brain and lays waste to all I've ever thought or experienced." He raised a teacherly finger. "Only this time, nothing will not give way to something. Just a flash, like sun on the windshield of a milk float, followed by nothing. I find the idea simultaneously awesome and terribly depressing."

"Maybe you ought to hold off for awhile," Robinson said. "You might..."

Timlin waited politely, eyebrows raised, his gun in one hand and his can of beer in the other.

"Fuck, I don't know," Robinson said. And then, surprising himself, he shouted, "*What did they do? What did those motherfuckers do?*"

"You're perfectly clear on what they did," Timlin said, "and now we live with the consequences. I know you love that dog, Peter. It's displaced love—substitute love—but we take what we can get, and if we've got half a brain, we're grateful. So don't hesitate. Stick him in the neck, and stick him hard. Grab his collar in case he flinches."

Robinson put his beer down. He didn't want it anymore. "He was in pretty bad shape when I left. Maybe he's dead already."

—⚍—

But he wasn't.

He looked up when Robinson came into the bedroom and thumped his tail twice on his sodden pad of blankets. Robinson sat down next to him. He stroked Gandalf's head and thought about the dooms of love, which were really so simple when you peered directly into them. Gandalf put his head on Robinson's knee and looked up at

# SUMMER THUNDER

him. Robinson took the hypo out of his shirt pocket and removed the protective cap from the needle.

"You're a good guy," he said, and took hold of Gandalf's collar, as Timlin had instructed. While he was nerving himself to go on, he heard a gunshot. The sound was faint at this distance, but with the lake so still, there was no mistaking it for anything else. It rolled across the quiet, diminished, tried to echo, failed. Gandalf cocked his ears, and an idea came to Robinson, as comforting as it was absurd. Maybe Timlin was wrong about the nothing. It was possible. In a world where you could look up and see stars, he reckoned anything was. Maybe they could find each other and go to the next thing together, just an old history teacher and his dog.

Gandalf was still looking at him as he slid the needle home. For a moment the dog's eyes remained bright and aware, and in the endless moment before the brightness left, Robinson would have taken it back if he could.

He sat there on the floor for a long time, hoping that last loon might sound off one more time, but it didn't. After awhile, he went out to the lean-to, found a spade, and dug a hole in his wife's flower garden. There was no need to go deep; no animal was going to come along and dig Gandalf up.

The next morning, Robinson's mouth tasted coppery. When he lifted his head, his cheek peeled away from the pillowcase. Both his nose and his gums had bled in the night.

It was another beautiful day, and although it was still summer, the first color had begun to steal into the trees. Robinson wheeled the Fat Bob out of the lean-to and replaced the dead battery, working slowly and carefully in the deep silence.

When he finished, he turned the switch. The green neutral light came on, but stuttered a little. He shut the switch off, tightened the connections, then tried again. This time the light stayed steady. He hit the ignition and the sound of summer thunder shattered the quiet. It seemed sacrilegious, but—this was strange—in a good way. Robinson wasn't surprised to find himself thinking of his first and only trip to attend the motorcycle rally that had been held in Sturgis every August. 1998 that had been, the year before he met Diana. He remembered rolling slowly down Junction Avenue on his Honda GB 500, one more sled in a parade of two thousand, the combined roar of all those bikes so loud it seemed a physical thing. Later that night there had been a bonfire, and an endless stream of Allman Brothers and AC/DC and Metallica roaring from Stonehenge stacks of Marshall amps. Tattooed girls danced topless in the firelight; bearded men drank beer from bizarre helmets; children decorated with decal tattoos of their own ran everywhere, waving sparklers. It had been terrifying and amazing and disgusting and wonderful, everything that was right and wrong with the world in the same place and in perfect focus. Overhead, a trillion stars.

Robinson gunned the Fat Boy, then let off the throttle. Gunned and let off. Gunned and let off. The rich smell of freshly burned gasoline filled the driveway. The world

# SUMMER THUNDER

was a dying hulk but the silence had been banished, at least for the time being, and that was good. That was fine. Fuck you, silence, he thought. Fuck you and the horse you rode in on. This is *my* horse, it's made of steel, and how do you like it?

He squeezed the clutch and toed the gearshift down into first. He rolled up the driveway, banked right, and toed up this time, into second and then third. The road was dirt, and rutted in places, but the bike took the ruts easily, floating Robinson up and down on the seat. His nose was spouting again; the blood streamed up his cheeks and flew off behind him in elongating droplets. He took the first curve and then the second, banking harder now, hitting fourth gear as he came onto a brief straight stretch. The Fat Bob was eager to go. It had been in that goddam lean-to for too long, gathering dust. On Robinson's right, he could see Lake Pocomtuc from the corner of his eye, still as a mirror, the sun beating a yellow-gold track across the blue. Robinson let out a yell and shook one fist at the sky—or maybe the universe—before returning it to the handgrip. Ahead was the buttonhook, and the sign reading MIND YOUR DRIVING! that marked Dead Man's Curve.

Robinson aimed for the sign and twisted the throttle all the way. He just had time to hit fifth gear.

# INCARNADINE

*Norman Partridge*

B AD THINGS HAPPEN IN THIS TOWN.
One of them happened tonight.
The man who did that thing stands on a bridge near the city limits. He has a pistol in his hand and a pack of cigarettes in his pocket. He can't decide which he wants in his mouth—a cigarette or the barrel of the .38. So he stands there in the dark, and he thinks about it, and he tries to make up his mind.

All that remains of the river below is a summertime trickle through cattails and garbage drowned by a long winter. Just a few blocks away, there's a house with a thrown breaker switch at the outside electrical box. Everything inside the house rests under a thick blanket of darkness, including two corpses gunned down with the killer's .38. There's more darkness than blood, but there's plenty of blood, too.

The killer never knew that a man and a woman could have so much blood in them, but this night has taught him the lesson. And though that blood no longer flows, he hears a red river of the stuff rushing through the night. This bit of sensory input, he believes, is a product of imagination. Reality says that there is no river here at all. Just the trickle of a dying creek. And cattails rustling quietly in the hot summer breeze. And garbage drowned by a long winter. And there are shadows, thick and heavy like the shadows in the house with the thrown breakers, because there is only a fingernail slice of moon slivered high in the sky tonight.

Yes. That's the way it is. The moon shines down on many other houses in this little town. The killer thinks about them, and about the people inside. He considers entering some of those houses with the .38 gripped in his hand. Though none in this town have wronged him as bad as the two lying dead in the darkness, others here have wronged him, and certainly. And he thinks of those people, and their houses, and the darkness that waits invitingly inside, ready to cover any action he might choose to take.

He follows the thought. He listens to the river, the one that isn't there. Suddenly, he is very tired. The moon above seems too much like a wound in the night, so he looks instead at the shadows welling beneath the bridge. These he sees for what they are, like the thoughts in his head. They are only shadows; there is no river of blood.

Still, the thoughts trouble him...as does the sound. It lingers. And that raw, salty smell—the night is steeped in it. A fine sheen of sweat moistens the killer's fingers, and the sweat brands the pistol. Suddenly, the end seems very near, and he wonders what it would be like to taste his own sweat while he pulled the pistol's trigger.

# INCARNADINE

He's tempted. Maybe too tempted. So he removes temptation. He drops the gun into the shadows. And just that fast, his heart begins thumping. He's not tired anymore. In fact, he feels a sudden rush of freedom. The sound below in the darkness is not quite a thud and not quite a splash, but it marks an ending. At least, the killer thinks it does. He lights a cigarette, but he doesn't even smoke half of it beneath the dull glow of the fingernail moon. Instead he flicks it into the shadows, watching the red dot of burning tobacco tumble through the darkness, hearing it hiss into a trickle of dank water as it joins the gun.

He hurries away from the shadows and the river that isn't there. By the time the cigarette is extinguished, the killer is in his car. He starts the engine and drives. And it's funny somehow. He's behind the steering wheel. His foot is on the gas. The road stretches before him, and the miles pile up behind him. The town where bad things happen grows distant, as does the blood on the floor in the house with the thrown breakers, as does the scent of that blood.

The killer is in a car, driving fast.

But he thinks only of a boat.

And a river called Charon.

So he drives faster.

Imagining the deserts that wait to the west.

—⁂—

The killer's pistol tumbles through the shadows, slowly, as if descending through the strong currents of a bloody sea. It lands in an old glove—open palm like an empty cradle; fingers curled and dried as if waiting to grasp.

A sharp slice of moonlight cuts between twisted oak branches and finds the gun and the glove. The pistol grips are still moist with the killer's sweat, and it dampens the old leather. Only slightly, but still...the killer's sweat is there, and it mingles with things unseen and unheard on the midnight wind. Magic rides that wind, too—rushing down the dry riverbed and invisible—but tangible nonetheless...and coming from a different source, soon to be revealed.

Yes. No fires burn and no cauldrons bubble, but there is magic here. This magic is born of blood. The fingers of the glove curl and close, driven by its power. That raw red scent lingers in the air, and the glove grasps it tightly.

A couple hundred yards up the dry riverbed, a young woman screams. Blood fills her mouth, and a splatter of red sprays the air as a fist connects with her jaw. Punches rain down on her like shadows, and the shadows are heavy with words. The woman hears them, and feels them, and bears their weight. But she can only bear so much. And the words and punches keep coming—an even, studied series as if well-practiced, searching for a particular result. Soon the woman's screams are almost a conditioned response, for (in many ways) it has always been this way for her.

The men are policemen. The woman is a witch. Of course, the men do not know this. They only know she's a hitchhiker who ended up on the wrong side of the city limits after dark. Besides, the woman has never been much of a witch, anyway. Her magic has always been born of necessity, and tentative in the worst way—the result of a few simple tools she carries in her backpack and a family heritage passed down by her grandmother. In the

# INCARNADINE

last week, her spells have been the simplest kind: 1) *That waitress will forget to bring me the bill,* and 2) *Tonight I am the only one who knows about Room 23 at the Tradewinds Motor Inn,* and 3) *Those cops won't see me hitchhiking...I am not even here.*

Of course, Spell Number Three did not work. If only it had. So now the witch is here at the edge of a dry riverbed, a quick sprint from a bridge she'll never travel and a possible escape she'll never make. The cops are almost finished with her. Her backpack is beneath her spine and useless, as is the minor magic it contains. But the blood is spilling—her blood—and that is something else indeed...a kind of magic of which, until now, she was unaware, a kind of magic she'd never dared touch for fear of some incalculable stain her grandmother had warned her against.

Of course, the witch never understood her grandmother's warnings. Not really. If she had...well, things might be different now. All things come with a price—especially strength. But perhaps that bit of understanding marks a beginning for the witch. For things are about to change for her, just as things have changed for the killer as he floors the gas pedal and races across a county line twenty miles distant. The road ahead of him is black, and his window is down to welcome the darkness, and (to him) the night still carries the music of a river, a deep one rushing behind him...with (perhaps) deeper water waiting ahead.

So the killer grips the steering wheel and imagines a tiller. Fading in and out of consciousness, the witch hears a river, too. And then other sounds stir in the night. They begin beneath the bridge, and the first of them is born of metal. A junked shopping cart begins to twist itself into a skeletal form, and the red bar touched by so many hands stretches as if reaching for one more until it reaches the glove that holds the killer's gun. The red plastic sheath covering that bar slivers and melts and five red fingers fill the glove. Slithers of old electrical wire weave like veins through a basket of red ribs. Soon a creature takes form, and a thing stands tall that never stood before. And though its roller-wheel feet aren't made for travel through cattails and garbage and muck, it creaks and capers a misshapen path to a junked Chrysler that spent the last winter underwater as a home for catfish.

Now, as summer wanes, the Chrysler is home for mosquitoes and centipedes. Of course, these creatures don't trouble the gloved shambler. It jams the killer's pistol through a pair of wire ribs, then pops the trunk with its gloved hand. Nothing much in there but an old jack buried under a rotted spare tire, but the jack will do.

The shambler bends low, and a wiry shoulder without an arm spills forth spider-web twists of red metal, weaving around the jack's notched armature, drawing it into a waiting socket. Now the shambler has another arm, a second one heavier than the first. The creature swings it. Tests it. And though it has no ears, the thing senses the metal whispering through the darkness, as silent as a slice of moonlight. A few more swings and the metal becomes malleable, as if finding a life of its own.

Another scream, a couple hundred yards up the dry riverbed.

Ready now, the thing shambles toward the ruckus.

# INCARNADINE

It does not have a head.

Not yet.

But a head is not important for the business at hand.

Besides, heads are easy to come by in a place like this.

After all, there is plenty of garbage waiting along the way.

—⚏—

"I think the fun's over with this one," says Officer Gordon.

"Naw. I don't think so," Officer Parks says. "Fact is, I think this little scag's ready to go another round. Ain't you, sweetie?"

No answer to that question. Parks laughs, wiping his raw knuckles on his uniform shirt. Christ, the laundry room in his house will probably look like a slaughterhouse tomorrow. And the back seat of the patrol car? Where they got started on the little scag? Oh, man. He's glad the night has plenty of shadows to blanket the nasty red Rorschach mess that must be hiding back there.

But, hey, that's the price of power. You want control, you're going to make a mess. That's a fact. Ain't no pretty pictures on the road to Top Dog territory. Parks learned that a long time ago, and he still believes it quite fervently. In fact, right now the thought's kind of comforting. Parks almost chuckles over it, but—

A different kind of laughter spills over his shoulder. It's like the metallic rasp of a saw, not amusing at all. Parks whirls to face it, drawing his pistol in the darkness, not understanding that even a draw that roughly matched the speed of lightning would be just a little too slow at this particular moment.

Because something is there behind him. Something… and it doesn't laugh like a man. There's just a slice of moonlight spilling down through the trees, but Parks can see that the thing is nearly on top of him. Christ. It's moving fast, and it looks like a skeleton, and its laughter echoes around him like a tin-can nightmare…and Jesus. The thing has a bucket for a head, a rusty bucket pocked with holes and—

—⚏—

The witch sees it all but believes none of it. She must be dreaming. The creature is made of metal and red…like blood. One of its arms—a tire jack—travels a deadly path. A straight shot—pulping the first cop's eyeball, driving straight through, shattering the bone behind the man's eye and carving a path through his brain.

The cop falls as the shambler steps past, its gloved metal fingers raising a pistol and firing. One, two, three quick (and precise) shots. Blood pours from the second cop's mouth as he topples. In the meantime, the shambler is still moving forward, because there is more work to be done.

The creature's glove is off now. Five sharp metal fingers gleam in the moonlight. Then the witch is gone for another moment. Unconscious. A flash fills her skull, like wild electricity, and her mind snaps back. Swollen eyes… blurry vision…but the witch sees the thing coming her way. Wiry gait. Clanking motion. Moonlight threading through its body like a sieve. A misplaced sculpture free of some mad museum…and a misplacer of time, too—for several more moments have vanished.

And then it happens again. Now the shambler is carrying the witch…now they are away from the trees and the riverbed…now they are climbing together on a switchback path that rises through the darkness. Yes. The clock has skipped a serious beat. The witch blinks, tries to speak through bruised lips, but words won't come. The thing moves forward, as if in a hurry. It wears both cops' badges now, clipped to the gridwork of its chest. And it has a head. She sees that. A rusty bucket pockmarked with holes, and…blood. Blood spills over the edges of the bucket, leaks through the pockmarked holes. And the witch hears things slapping wetly within the bucket—things the creature harvested from the dead cops down by the riverbed.

A brain, no doubt… and maybe a heart. Again, the witch fades. The wiry shambler inclines its bucket head, and blood spills on her face, and blood awakens her.

*Drip drip drip,* she thinks. *This is how it starts. And then the dam begins to break, like dams always do. And then the river—*

The witch screams, one last time. No longer in the creature's arms. Afraid where she might be. Because time is spinning like a plate balanced on a stick. Time is beginning to tumble like that very same plate ready to hit the floor. She's on a picnic table now, beneath a sky littered with stars, near a twisting, narrow road. In the distance—houses, city streets. The bucket-headed thing stands above her, bending over…almost solicitously. *Drip drip drip.*

Blood rains down. The witch looks up, red trickles on her face. The thing does not move. The badges on its chest gleam in the moonlight. The creature defies easy description. Not quite a skeleton. Not quite a scarecrow. Not quite hero or monster.

A walking shadow, she thinks.

*A walking shadow.*

And, then, quite suddenly, the witch drifts away.

Past the place where shadows dwell.

Into the waiting embrace of true darkness.

—⚉—

Bucket Head stands over the witch. The arm built from a jack is gone. It has been replaced with a shotgun. The basket of the thing's pelvis, likewise, has been repurposed. Once that basket held children while shopping. Now it holds several .38's, none of them secured with a requisite safety strap.

Of course, none of these things can help a witch who has slipped into a coma. Bucket Head does not understand this. Understanding is not in the creature's basic skill-set. Still, it tries to rouse her but is unable. So it takes hold of the witch's arm, and it pulls her off the bench, and it drags her to the patrol car. These actions seem correct, and Bucket Head considers no others. Quiet calculation is not the shambler's game, for it is a creature born from a killer's cursed gun and witch's dream. Not human at all, but like men and women everywhere it has a set of parents. The thing its parents share is blood, and this is what they have given Bucket Head.

Yes. Blood is the creature's heritage, and blood is its future. This is all Bucket Head knows. Two dead men in its

# INCARNADINE

wake, but there are many houses ahead. Thick blankets of darkness. Outside breaker switches waiting to be thrown. A whole town full of them. Those who wronged a killer; those who would wrong a witch. A whole town…just waiting for Bucket Head.

The creature opens the rear door of the squad car. The witch's blood has dried on the seats. Bucket Head slides her across the upholstery. She draws a shallow breath. A sign of life. This is important, as important as the deaths of others.

Bucket Head slams the door and climbs behind the wheel.

Metal fingers key the ignition. Headlights flare, cutting through the night.

Just ahead, hell is murky.

Bucket Head drives toward it.

—⚡—

The police cruiser's motor is well-tuned, and it purrs like a contented panther. In the backseat, the witch drifts deeper into a coma, and deeper still.

Headlights cut through the night as the patrol car advances on the town where bad things happen. The witch hears the river behind her, rushing away in the distance. Rushing, and not in reverie. The sound takes her, as does the river. Suddenly she's floating…as if swept away on a fast current. The current is red, and it is hers, in the same way that everything in this night is hers except the killer and his gun. And it carries her quickly and safely, just as Bucket Head carried her, for this river is the creature's brother. It washes beneath a bridge where a killer once stood, and it fills the night like great Neptune's ocean, and not all the perfumes of Arabia could sweeten the smell of its salty stench.

The river is here, and it is everywhere. In this moment, it rushes as surely as the blood that fills the witch's veins. Red and rich, it wells around the tires of a killer's car as he races across a state line to the west, and it rises from storm-drains in the streets of the town he left behind, and very soon it will spill across the floor of a dark house with thrown breakers where two corpses wait.

Yes. The river is rising…and fast.

Here and everywhere.

Blood, after all, will have blood.

## THE WESTERN DEAD

*Jack Ketchum*

"Shoot 'em in the head, for lord's sake," said Sam Pitts.

"Sometimes I like to play 'em a little," said Chunk Colbert.

"It's a waste of munitions."

"Munitions we got. It's women we don't got."

Chunk was always going on about the women and Sam had to allow he was right about that however annoying it was to be reminded of the fact morning, noon, and night. Apache aside, the closest women around were the Widow Heller a mile up the Gila and the wife and daughter of Lonesome Charley McSween halfway back to Fort Thomas. Charley's Etta was a sight to see and the daughter was burgeoning fine but the Widow Heller could frighten a prairie rattler back into its burrow.

He wondered how any of them were doing.

Sam and Chunk and Doc Cleveland sat beneath the timid shade of the thatched roof ramada and in the glare of sun and baked adobe watched the White Mountain Apache whose left front forearm Chunk's Colt Army .44 had just now retired to the dirt hobble toward them across the quadrangle, mouth working like he sensed it was suppertime. Which Sam supposed he did.

Chunk fired again and a good-sized hole appeared in the Apache's breechcloth.

"Goddamn!" said Doc. "You shot off that fella's wedding tackle! That's it, right there behind him."

"You're the doc, Doc," said Chunk. "You ought to know. I'm gettin' pretty good at that shot in particular."

"Quit foolin' 'round, Chunk," said Sam. "Else I'll take him with the Spencer."

At a range this close the Spencer would make one helluva mess.

"Awww, alright, Sam, if you say so."

He took a pull on the bottle of Forty-Rod whiskey and squinted into the sun and aimed and fired. The Apache went down like an oatsack, the top of his head three feet back. Sam had to admire Chunk's skill with both the Colt and the whiskey. Forty-Rod was nothing more than pure alcohol colored with coffee or burnt sugar and forty rods was about as far as a man could walk before paralysis made further movement unlikely for a while. But Chunk had been at it all morning while they sat there shooting dead White Mountain warriors and the occasional squaw.

"Kinda slow today, Sam, doncha think?"

"'Lot fewer than yesterday this time of day. And no three or four at once. Why's that do you suppose?"

"I dunno. They drifted on?"

"Maybe."

Still they had well over a dozen bodies littering the quadrangle. Come the blessed cool of evening they'd pile them into the wagon and haul them out of the station against the rot and stink. But not for a while yet.

Right now the day was hot as a whorehouse on nickel night.

In ordinary circumstances this was the kind of chore he'd have left to the Coyotero Apache scouts. There were forty-two of them under Sam's command. But the scouts had all lit out under cover of darkness three nights ago. The same day dead White Mountain Apaches started showing up at their door with a powerful yearning for human flesh be it Coyotero flesh or white man.

They'd learned this lack of partiality the hard way.

Mata Lobo had been his number one scout before going out to greet Leaning Crow coming down from the reservation that morning and getting his neck bit in half for his trouble. Then Will Fry, his interpreter and longtime friend, rode out to the wickiups three miles downriver to see what the devil was going on with their two hundred or thereabouts native charges. Saw a young naked girl in the cottonwoods and prickly pear and got off his pony. Got right back on again when the girl bit off a chunk of his gunhand between thumb and forefinger and rode back into Gila Camp bleeding all over his good chestnut mare.

They'd telegraphed for Doc but by the time Doc's stage arrived they'd already had to put a bullet in Will's head. Same as Leaning Crow and Mata Lobo. Doc said he'd seen it once before with a trooper who'd been bit on the shoulder just outside of Fort Thomas and knew it was going to be useless riding out there. But he and Will were friends too from way back so you did what you had to do. Yet Sam figured it was that—the plain solid fact that if these damn things bit you *anywhere* you were gone home to Boston so to speak—that spooked his Coyoteros.

Now Doc was waiting on transportation—either the stage back to the Fort or the cavalry, whichever came first. The cavalry was late mustering—they'd been sent for two days ago—and the stage was late as always. But Doc was no fool. He was not riding out of there without company.

Meantime they shot Apaches.

"Tell us that yarn again, Doc," said Chunk. "I ain't likely to believe it any more this time than I did yesterday but it'll serve to pass the time."

"You mean about the Egyptian or Frank Shirley?"

"The Eye-gyptian. Any man gets his steel hard by having his wife stand against a wall whilst he shoots her figure in the goddamn plaster don't deserve a re-telling."

Doc nodded. "Terhan Bey. He told me that's where they come from. These dead folks. Come from Egypt originally. He says they been around since long before the Lord His Own Self. Says it's all his people's fault."

"What was this Bey fella's complaint again?" said Sam.

"Ear abscess. Amused me no end, I'll tell you. Here's this snake-oil salesman scared to imbibe his own tonic."

"Apache use a few drops of piss," said Chunk.

"I'm told it can work," said Doc. "Never tried it. Anyhow, we're talking here about the pharaohs. According to this Bey fella, the *first real* pharaoh. United the upper and lower kingdoms. Whole of Egypt. Gentleman by the name of Narmer or Narner, I forget. Bey called him the Scorpion King. And he sure did have a sting to him."

"Scorpions? They got those damn creatures in Egypt?"

"Why not? You got to figure that the land ain't much different than what we got here. Desert mostly. Houses mostly mud. Hot days and wicked cold nights. 'Course we got the Gila here while they got the Nile. Whole lot bigger, more powerful. You fellas at all familiar with any of this?"

Sam shook his head. The Doc was an educated man and Sam felt the lack. Chunk just grunted.

"I saw a statue of one of these pharaohs at the old Arsenal building up in New York City. Natural history museum now. Held a crook and a flail."

"Flail? Like a thresher you mean?" said Sam.

"That's right. Flail says that he's provider of food for his people. And the crook's like a shepherd's crook, says he's his peoples' shepherd. Seems old Narmer or Narner shepherded his people into some pretty strange places if you believe Terhan Bey."

"Here's where I start *dis*believin'," said Chunk.

"You think what you want, Chunk. But the way he tells it, Narmer's also the first to start seekin' after life eternal. Life everlasting. Though here's where it gets a bit confusing to my mind. This pharaoh, they *already* call him God. His people do. I asked Bey about that. If he's God, don't he already have life everlasting?"

"Good question, Doc."

"I thought so, Chunk. Bey said it was their feeling that it was the pharaoh and the pharaoh's power that held the sky up and made the river rise. Damn big responsibility. So they venerated him as a god."

"Venerated?"

"Like in church, Chunk. When you pray to the cross."

Sam thought it unlikely that Chunk had ever been inside a church but kept that to his chest and rolled himself a Bull Durham.

"But this Narmer fella didn't *feel* like God. Felt pretty mortal I guess. So he set his soldiers and priests to experimentin.'"

"There's another one, Sam. You see him there?"

"I do."

The man was naked as the day he was born and that was unlike the Apache who among the men at least tended to want to cover their loins. He was rounding the corner from the livery stable and inside horses snorted at his presence. Sam allowed that an Apache did have a stink to him dead or not.

"Ain't that Standing Water?" said Chunk.

"I believe it is," said Sam.

Many that day had come at them unarmed but Standing Water had been a rough bit of work while alive and was almost bound to be so dead. Anyway the knife in his hand was clear enough glinting in the sun. Like pretty much all of them he was staggering mouth ajar toward the ramada but he was moving a bit faster than most. Already Sam could see that he was bit on the shoulder and that this was what had put him down.

He didn't want Chunk fooling with him. He raised the Spencer and fired once and all was still again.

"Nice one," said Chunk. "So you were saying?"

"The experiments, yes. You truly want to hear this again?"

# THE WESTERN DEAD

"Sure I do."

"You're of a gruesome nature, Chunk."

Doc sighed.

"They had the notion that you'd find the secret to life eternal in one of only a few places—in the loins of the male or female, in the heart or in the blood. So they shed a lot of blood, both slave and freeman. Did a whole lot of rapin'. And not just the ladies but the men and children too, Chunk. Took a whole lot of hearts and privates from their rightful owners.

"I guess they felt that dying itself might hold a kind of magic to it and that you might get a harness on that by prolonging the process if you know what I mean. Though personally I don't see that. F'rinstance, you got to know that when Yellow Horse and his boys hung old Sam Stark upside down over that slow fire he must have begged for a bullet in the brain. You're in that much pain, you don't care to live forever. But they tried it anyway. So you got your crucifixion, your impalement, your vivisection."

"What's a vividsection?"

"No letter d, Chunk. Vivisection. Take a body apart whilst it's still breathin'."

"You can do that?"

"Real carefully. They tried all kinds of tricks, Bey said. The carpenter come by with his chisel, the stonecutter come by with his drill, the baker with his yeast, the brewer with his malt. Used cobwebs or soot against the blood. Used knitbone, mad stone, nettles, goose grease, beeswax, mustard. All manner of stuff."

"This vivisec thing. How you handle that exactly?"

"Well, you know how a Comanche or rogue Apache will scalp a fella and unless they slit his throat in the bargain or he loses too much blood there ain't no reason he won't be right as rain in a few weeks or so? Same thing with body parts. Arm, leg, pecker, eyeball. All you got to do is cauterize and watch out for arteries. You can cut a man open and remove an organ, long as it ain't the heart or brain. You cauterize. You can drill through bone. Plenty of things you can do to a man without killin' him. Take all day if you've got a mind to. But I digress.

"The fella behind all this mayhem was a gentleman name of Abydos, servant in Narmer's palace. A freeman, not a slave—and one with ambitions. Which in time he did overreach. 'Cause for a long while he was overseeing priest and soldier alike in all this nasty business and enjoying every minute of it, then next thing you know he's on the receiving end."

Doc paused in his storytelling. A little girl perhaps six years of age shuffled unsteady into the quadrangle past the now-empty bunkhouse the Coyotero had abandoned, her entrails trailing like a muddy rope. Chunk shot and kicked up dirt in front of her. Sam levered a bullet into the Spencer's chamber and aimed more carefully than Chunk had and the girl's head exploded.

"I hate to see that," said Doc. "The little 'uns."

"'Nother good one, though," said Chunk.

"Thanks. Hadn't you better reload that weapon of yours, Chunk?" He nodded toward the Colt. "You never know."

"You have a point," said Chunk.

# THE WESTERN DEAD

He threw open the cylinder and reached for the powder at his feet. Changed his mind and reached for the Forty-Rod instead and drank deep from the bottle. Put the bottle down and this time found his powder.

"Get to the part about the daughter, Doc," he said.

"Give me some of that Forty-Rod, Chunk."

Chunk did. Doc drank.

"This Abydos had a daughter. Little thing. Twelve, maybe thirteen years of age. In his high ambition he figured that maybe the gods might favor him should he volunteer her for one of the experiments of theirs. Nothing else had been working out for him exactly. So in front of his very eyes that little girl was raped again and again by the pharaoh's soldiers and tortured for days on end. Her breasts and private parts in particular, for the obvious reasons. Seats of life, right? He was there to hear her every scream."

"That's one evil sonovabitch," said Chunk.

Sam took note. It seemed that for the moment at least Chunk had ceased his disbelieving.

"That he was, Chunk, that he was. Most evil fella in the land by then and no doubt about it. Sold his soul to the very Devil's what I'd say. No telling what he'd been like in days prior—though I'd wager he couldn't ever have been much—but evil can transform a man. And this Abydos was way over halfway to transformin'.

"But see now, pharaoh had himself a daughter too. And bloodthirsty as he was he didn't much care for the notion of a daddy using his own blood kin that way. Didn't seem right to him I imagine. Abydos had been pretty much a failure anyway. So he ordered the fella chained to a wall and treated pretty much the way they'd treated his daughter for a few days and at long last ordered his daughter's head stove in, right in front of him. And the rest must have been some sort of divine inspiration.

"'Cause they made him drink of her blood and eat of her flesh. And when he was finished they stabbed him through the heart.

"He died a'course—and then he *didn't* die. Because he'd long since turned that blind eye of his to all human pain and grief and sorrow, even his own daughter's pain and grief and sorrow, because he'd damned himself down to the bone, humanity was lost to this gentleman even in death. He rose and walked the mud and sands again. With nothing inside but a hunger to infect every living creature he touched with the self-same evil he carried deep within. And pharaoh had his secret to eternal life."

They saw dust rise. Far off in the bleak horizon.

"Coach?" said Doc.

"If I had to judge, I'd say cavalry," said Sam. "'That's a good bit of dust. 'Bout time."

He thought of his own daughter, his own wife, far away in Louisville. He felt shame at his own betrayal which was so much smaller than Abydos' but betrayal nonetheless. And him become some Indian agent in this heat-struck hell of nowhere.

"They called him *Ka*," said the Doc. "Egyptian word for life-force or soul or something on that order. Bey was never clear. But I guess Ka had his uses after all. Raised up a whole damn army of the dead to do the pharaoh's bidding."

The horses snorted. Sam looked left and right and saw nothing but the flat baked squat adobe buildings

# THE WESTERN DEAD

and the quadrangle in which many had died yet a second time this day and yesterday and the day before and the shimmering heatwaves and dust off the flatlands and the dim blue mountains beyond.

"I still don't get it, Doc," said Chunk. "Egypt's a damn far piece away, right? Even if this Bey fella's tellin' you the god's honest truth. How'd they get here? I mean, *here?* On some Apache reservation. You know what I'm sayin'?"

Doc shrugged and pulled on the whiskey again.

"Evil can travel quite a ways in a few hundred years, Chunk. It can travel many a mile."

And events were to confirm this. For Sam was right.

It was indeed the cavalry which approached them nearly sixty strong and Apache among them too following their brief skirmish. Soldiers and White Mountain Apache mountless and dead to a man.

Chunk proved to be wrong about the adequate munitions.

# AN INSTANT ETERNITY

*Brian James Freeman*

"In life there is not time to grieve long
But this, this is out of life, this is out of time,
An instant eternity of evil and wrong."
— T.S. Eliot, *Murder in the Cathedral*

WHEN STEPHEN SPOTTED THE LITTLE GIRL HIDING IN the doorway of the crumbling house, he was certain his daughter had somehow snuck along.

The idea made no sense. Rebecca was safe at home on the other side of the world, far from this war torn wasteland. She hadn't been on the never-ending overseas military transport flight and she certainly wasn't staying in the Green Zone hotels or riding in the U.N.'s white helicopters to cover possible news stories.

But as strange as that first thought was, the realization that someone—anyone—was watching them didn't make a lot of sense, either.

No one was supposed to be in this abandoned town. The escorted group of reporters, photographers, and cameramen wore paper masks provided by the U.N.'s media liaison team and they wouldn't be here for long. There had been no sign of any civilians when the helicopters circled the region on the way in and they didn't expect to see anyone on the way out. Only the insane and the sick would still be living here. The few locals who had ventured into the valley called this place "the devil's hands." That's where you'd find yourself if you stayed too long, they said.

Stephen carried his camera in his hands, ready for any spontaneous shot that might happen in the blink of an eye, and he walked alongside Rick McDuff, the reporter he was working with on this assignment. Together they were lagging behind the rest of the group, talking quietly and noting items of interest, possible angles for stories others might not notice.

Rick had a great eye for a unique hook to catch the reader's attention. His career dated clear back to Vietnam and nothing fazed him anymore. Stephen wished he could say the same, but he was merely a self-taught photographer on his first tour of duty outside his hometown and he didn't have the courage or the stomach for horrific scenes like Rick did.

Stephen did a double take when he spotted the little girl. She appeared in the doorway of the crumbling house after the other reporters passed by and her hesitant movement caught Stephen's eye. A dirty and tattered dress was draped over her skeletal frame. Her skin was pale and her eyes were very blue.

"Rick, check that out," Stephen said, pointing as the girl ducked back into the rubble that had once been a home.

"The house?"

"No, the little girl."

"I don't see anyone," Rick said. He glanced at Stephen for a moment and then back at the empty, ruined house. "They searched to make sure the area was clear, you know."

Stephen didn't reply, but he watched the house closely as they passed by. He didn't see any other sign of movement or occupation, no indication of life at all.

The valley rose around what had once been a thriving community of a thousand people. Nearby was the decaying nuclear power plant on the river, the focus of the media's visit today. Summer sunlight reflected off the water and heat waves shimmered over what remained of the paved roads. Much of the forest was growing back, reclaiming everything it could, but there were still large sections of land scarred by the government's massive carpet-bombing of the rebel army.

The U.N. had needed four cargo helicopters to transport the reporters for today's series of ready-made news stories, and this town was the last stop on the tour. So far they had visited an overpopulated refugee camp, a motorcycle factory converted into a military headquarters during the war, and a water treatment plant bombed back to the Stone Age by one of the many rebel factions.

Stephen was in a competitive profession—getting an original shot was tough even when you took hundreds or thousands of digital photos every day—but he hated the way his colleagues treated these location visits like a group of tourists on vacation. Being in this terrible wasteland was pushing Stephen to his limits.

Whenever he closed his eyes, he saw the scarred bodies of children burned by the bombings; he saw grieving widows; he saw houses that would never be homes again; he saw men and boys and women and girls missing limbs.

Other people's lives echoed through his thoughts like ghosts. Every burned-out car in the middle of a street told a story. Every collapsed building. Every rotting skeleton on a scarred sidewalk. Every improvised burial site.

Stephen knew he wasn't supposed to get emotional about these things—it was his work, his business, his job—but the horrors had begun to haunt his nights. Sometimes, during the worst of the nightmares, he couldn't even tell if he was awake or asleep.

When Stephen was a teenager, his father had once told him that death was actually a single moment of eternity and there was nothing you could do in that moment but accept your fate. If your time was up, your time was up. Back then Stephen had thought his father was being melodramatic, but not anymore.

Terror and death were everywhere all around him, all the time, whether his eyes were open or closed, and he just wanted to go home to be with his family, to leave this land of destruction behind forever.

Although he could speak with Tracy and Rebecca almost every evening via the Internet video chat, it wasn't the same, it wasn't enough. He wanted to experience all the important moments in their lives he was missing. He wanted to hold them again. He never wanted to let them go, not ever.

Soon Stephen *would* be headed home, though. A truce between the rebels and the government had been signed, so his work here was almost finished. Readers were losing interest, too. Stories about the aftermath of the war and the rebuilding effort weren't getting nearly as many hits on the newspaper's website.

But until the big bosses at the paper said he was done, Stephen had a job to do and he wanted to do it the best he could.

The herd of reporters entered the old town square overgrown with wild grasses and bushes badly in need of tending. In the center of the square was a tall statue of a soldier, but almost no one in the group paid the monument any attention. They could now see the power plant's four concrete towers in the distance. Everyone murmured excitedly.

Everyone except for Stephen, who was studying the ruins around the town square, searching for anyone else who might be hiding and watching them. Insects buzzed around his head and the sunlight beat against his face. He felt disconnected from the world. Everything around him seemed to be shifting one step away from reality and then taking one big step back.

*I need to get out of here,* Stephen thought. *I have to submit my request for reassignment before it's too late or I might never leave this country.*

He closed his eyes. When he opened them again, he felt a little better. He just had to make it through this one last stop on today's tour of horrors and then they'd be headed back to the Green Zone and the hotel.

At least their visit to this town would be quick. Several times they had been cautioned about the continuing danger from the radiation. Fear guaranteed they wouldn't stick around too long.

They were also frequently reminded by their guides of how the United Nations had dramatically flown into the Hot Zone after the power plant's meltdown to evacuate the community, losing two helicopters in the process. One had exploded on the ground and the other had been shot down by a rebel's surface-to-air missile stolen from an old military stockpile, but in the end, hundreds of townspeople had been saved.

The anniversary of the heroic rescue was the prepackaged story for this leg of the media field trip. Most of the journalists would run with it. Using the prepared news was easier than digging for something deeper, and in the end, you got paid the same either way.

The reporters stomped forward through the overgrown grasses of the town square to get a better look at the power plant, but this was as far as they could go. The road beyond the square was a live minefield.

An advance team had left a row of red cones marked with international warning signs on the pavement. "Past this point awaits death" was the gist, no matter what your language. There were also rows of red flags indicating the locations of several mines right after the cones, just to make sure the point was loud and clear. The advance team would have only marked the mines closest to where the visitors might be, though. There could be (and probably

# AN INSTANT ETERNITY

were) many more long forgotten explosive devices beyond the town square.

Twenty yards into the danger zone were the shredded remains of the U.N. helicopter that had exploded during the town's evacuation. The burnt and twisted metal had rusted with the passage of time.

Next to the helicopter was a wrecked pick-up truck. The tires were flat and the bed and cab were spotted with holes from the improvised explosive device that had ripped it apart. The windows of the nearby apartment building were shattered and the bricks were dotted with shrapnel.

As Stephen wiped the sweat away from his eyes, he studied the group he was traveling with. They were taking pictures and making notes, joking with each other in a variety of languages while standing next to a monument dedicated to the town's war dead from the nation's past conflicts. The whole idea of what they were doing in this devastated place felt surreal.

"Think you should take some more shots, Mr. Photographer?" Rick asked, scribbling a few names off the monument into his notebook.

Stephen recognized the angle Rick had chosen for his report and he started snapping photographs to illustrate it: the tall monument from a low view, the remains of the wooden fence that once surrounded the town square, and the charred framework of the burned buildings. When possible, he included the four concrete towers looming in the distance.

Actually, with the camera's zoom lenses, he could see the old power plant quite well. The island's native vegetation had already overgrown the buildings and the ivy and vines would camouflage the towers before too long.

Stephen turned away and snapped photographs of a rusted car sitting in the middle of the street with all four doors open. The seats had been partially devoured by the weather and a flowering plant was growing out of the back window. Not a bad shot, but nothing special. He had seen it a thousand times before.

"Okay, time to return to our rides," the lead media liaison announced in his thick accent. "As we take off, try to imagine what it felt like for all the townspeople who were rescued from certain death in some of these same helicopters."

"You get the shots you wanted?" Rick asked while he packed up his notebook for the flight back to the Green Zone base where they'd spend the night.

"I have enough," Stephen replied. He stood by the monument while everyone else dutifully filed back to the street, which would take them to the field outside of town where the helicopters waited, their powerful engines still revved and ready to go.

He was the last person standing in the overgrown town square. He took a final shot of the lonely remains of the destroyed rescue helicopter before he started back athrough the tall grasses.

As he neared the cracked road out of town, something hidden at the edge of the grass reflected a ray of sunlight. He knelt and picked up a silver necklace and held it above his head. The chain with the crucifix was probably very old, possibly a treasured gift that had been passed from mother to daughter.

# AN INSTANT ETERNITY

Stephen slipped the necklace into his pocket and he glanced around, expecting Rick to be waiting for him, but the group was already nearing the top of the hill, more than two blocks away. No one had noticed that he wasn't with them.

A slight wave of panic rose inside of Stephen, but he found that he couldn't move. His legs were like marble and he didn't understand why.

He thought he heard a voice on the breeze brushing past him. Someone calling for him from the group? No, the sound was behind him.

He looked toward the power plant and there she was. The little girl.

She was standing in the middle of the street, her wide eyes showing her terror. She remained motionless a few feet from the pick-up truck as their eyes met.

She was as real as anyone Stephen had ever seen. He turned toward the reporters and U.N. personnel walking briskly over the hill.

"Hey, wait a minute!" he yelled. He jumped in the air, waving his arms. "Hey, you guys!"

No one responded. They obviously couldn't hear him over the noise from the revving helicopters.

"Please help me," the little girl called.

Stephen hurried to the edge of the town square where the red cones and warning signs awaited him. He took a good look at the street and the sidewalks lining it.

Hundreds of mortar shells had peppered the street during the war and the holes left behind from the explosions were eventually filled with dirt. Those dirt sections—some large, some small, some nearly the width of the street—seemed to be where the mines had been planted, at least based on the location of the red flags around the town square.

Stephen turned again to the group of people topping the hill.

"Hey!" he screamed as he jumped and frantically waved his arms. The group kept moving like they had already forgotten the town.

"Please," the little girl whimpered.

Stephen knew there wasn't any time to waste. He took a deep breath and stepped past the cones and the warning signs, moving slowly, making sure his shoes connected with firm pavement. When he reached the little girl, he dropped to one knee so they were both about the same height. Her skin was dirty and her eyes wide.

"I need help," she said very quietly, as if she was afraid to raise her voice.

"Come here," Stephen said, taking her small hand into his own. Her bright blue eyes were filled with tears. Her gaunt skin was tight against her bones. "I'll take you to the helicopters and they'll fly you to safety."

"No!" The little girl yanked her hand free, but she didn't attempt to run away.

"We need to go right now."

"I can't."

"Why not?"

With a trembling hand, the little girl pointed at her battered tennis shoes, which were speckled with dried blood. She was standing on a slight mound of dirt that had shifted under her weight.

"I heard it click," she whispered.

# AN INSTANT ETERNITY

"Oh shit."

Stephen stood and looked toward the top of the hill. He saw no one. He could hear the rotors speeding up as the helicopters prepared to leave.

In his panic, he took a step without thinking, almost started to run, but then he remembered where he was and he stopped cold. Between him and safety were all those holes filled with dirt, the red flags near the town square, the cones with their warning signs facing away from him. He was definitely on the wrong side of the safe zone.

"Please don't leave me," the little girl whispered.

"I have to get some help. Don't move, okay? Not one inch. I'll be right back. I promise I won't leave you here."

Stephen's quick footsteps were carefully placed as he navigated his way past where he believed the mines had been buried. His eyes were locked on the ground and sweat poured off his face.

By the time he reached the town square, the first helicopter had risen above the tree line. If Stephen was lucky, they'd fly his way and someone would spot him. Even if they flew in the other direction, he should still be okay, though. The U.N. media liaisons were supposed to do a head count on each helicopter, just to be safe. When they did that, they would realize they were one person short and they'd count again.

Stephen knew he couldn't depend on Rick to realize his photographer was missing since they had ridden on different helicopters at least twice today and there was no assigned seating, but one of the media liaisons would notice. They'd have to notice. Taking care of the journalists was their job, after all.

Stephen raced across the town square while the other two helicopters rose into the sky. They headed south, away from the town.

"Dammit," he whispered, breaking into a sprint, pushing himself as hard as he could, his legs churning under him, his camera swinging around his neck. He had been a track and field star in high school, winning several races at the regional level and even finishing in the top three for the high jump twice, but he hadn't stayed in that kind of shape since he married and entered the workforce.

Stephen reached the top of the hill where the town's main street became a winding road that passed by a creek and the U.N.'s improvised landing field before twisting into the woods and continuing to an old highway five miles away. He started down the other side of the hill as the last helicopter lifted off.

"Hey! Hey, you idiots! You were supposed to count!" he screamed, running toward the field of overgrown grass and forgotten farm equipment. The helicopter continued up and then turned south, following the first three. Stephen jumped and waved his arms like a madman, but still, no one saw him.

"No, dammit! Down here!"

The last helicopter vanished over the hills, the sound of the rotors quickly fading away. Stephen was left standing alone in the field full of muddy boot prints, trampled weeds, and abandoned tractors. A candy wrapper blew past him on the summer breeze.

*Dammit, God dammit,* Stephen thought, rushing back to town. He topped the hill and was relieved to see the little girl hadn't moved. His legs were beginning to ache, but he didn't slow until he reached the memorial in the town square.

He stopped and lifted his camera, focused on the girl, and snapped a couple of shots. If for some reason he didn't make it back, he wanted his photographs to survive. They would tell the story of what had happened. He placed his camera on the wooden bench near the statue.

"You're going to be okay," Stephen called to the girl as he carefully navigated his way to where she stood. "Stay very, very still. I'll get you out of here."

"Please don't leave me again," the little girl whispered, her voice trembling.

"I won't." Stephen knelt in front of her, wiped her tears away. "What's your name?"

"Lilly." Her voice cracked. Her legs were shaking.

"That's a pretty name. Listen to me, Lilly. You can't move. Do you understand?"

She nodded.

"You heard something click when you stepped on the dirt?"

"Yes. The bad click. Like the one that killed my Mommy. The one Daddy taught me about."

"How did you get here? Where's your father now?"

"Daddy's a soldier."

"Does he wear a uniform?"

"Before Mommy died."

"What about after your mom died?"

"Daddy took me and my brothers to some cabins in the woods with some other soldiers."

*Oh shit,* Stephen thought. *Her father joined one of the rebel groups.*

"Then they went to fight the bad men and they never came back."

"How long have they been gone?"

"Since winter. I came here to find them."

Stephen thought about the last major offensive against the rebels before the truce, five months ago. That battle wasn't too far from this town, maybe ten miles, just outside the capitol city. One last stand on the bloody riverbanks and small islands, a night of gunfire and explosions and bloodshed. He shot a lot of graphic photos afterwards, far too graphic to appear in the legitimate news, but there were plenty of websites that would have bought them if he had been selling. He had deleted most of the photos at the hotel that same night.

When Stephen looked at this little girl, he saw the bodies and the blood and the destruction on the riverbanks. He didn't even have to close his eyes. He might have photographed her brothers or her father for all he knew.

"Mommy died over there," Lilly said, pointing. "We were walking to the market and a bomb in the ground clicked and she told me to get away real fast."

"I'm sorry," Stephen said. He put his hands on his knees to steady himself against a wave of dizziness. The street was so damn hot. The tar in the pavement's cracks was bubbling and the heat shimmered in the air like dancing phantoms. His armpits were damp and his pulse was racing; he could hear his heart beating in his ears. His fingers shook, just a little.

"Please help me," Lilly whispered. Her resemblance to Rebecca was scary and Stephen had to stop himself from calling her by the wrong name. "Daddy told me not

# AN INSTANT ETERNITY

to move if I heard a click when I was walking. He said he'd help me."

"It's good you didn't move. Are you sure you heard a click?"

"Yes. Like Mommy's."

"No problem, Lilly, you're going to be okay. Trust me."

She nodded, believing him in the way children are trained to believe adults, but then, before she could speak again, her body began to sway and her eyelids fluttered, her eyes bulged and rolled. Her arms swooped outward, her legs bent at the knees, and she started to collapse.

Stephen reached out and caught Lilly by the arm and he held her so her weight was still on her legs.

For the longest moment of his life, Stephen was certain they were about to die. If her weight shifted too much, the mine would explode and they'd both be killed. But he held her and eventually she began to blink and she glanced around, startled and dazed.

"What happened?" she asked, groggy, like she had been awakened from a deep sleep.

"Are you okay?"

"Sorry," she whispered. "I got dizzy. I'm so thirsty."

"It's okay," he said. "I can get you some water."

But he couldn't. Not here. This whole area was poison. There wasn't any clean water anywhere, and even if there was, he couldn't leave this little girl alone in her condition. Instead he kept holding her while he searched for a solution and he didn't say anything else until she finally spoke again.

"I'm so tired."

"You need to stay still, but don't worry, you'll be okay."

Stephen's mind was running red hot, trying to remember any relevant events he had witnessed in this war, any of the countless stories Rick had told him in the countless hotel bars. Stephen had seen a lot of people killed by mines since he came to this country. Stepping in the wrong place in the wrong field, driving on the wrong road. Once he had watched from a distance as a U.N. bomb disposal unit attempted to disarm a mine buried in the middle of a schoolyard. The men were blown to pieces. They had been pros. They were dead.

Stephen wiped more sweat and tears away from the little girl's face. Considering how exhausted she was and given the situation, he thought she was holding herself together pretty well. Better than some adults he had seen. Maybe because she truly believed there was a way out of the situation, some means to fix this problem. She didn't know the truth like he did.

"Do you know what kind of bomb it is, Lilly? Did your father ever mention that?"

Her eyes had grown glassy, but Stephen's words seemed to wake her up a bit. She whispered, "It hops."

*It hops.*

A hopping bomb. He knew what she meant. Rick had called them Bouncing Betties. They were quite popular for the rebels in this war thanks to all of the Army depots that had been overrun in the early days of the fighting. There were millions of these things littering the landscape, hibernating under the dirt, just waiting to release their explosive fury.

A very specific memory returned to Stephen: Rick in some hotel bar explaining that a Bouncing Betty was designed to launch into the air after a soldier activated it, detonating approximately three seconds later so the explosion would rip apart a whole group of soldiers instead of maiming or killing just one.

But those three seconds gave Stephen an idea.

As the idea took shape, a voice that sounded very much like his own whispered to him: *You're fucking kidding yourself, Stephen. You don't even know if the kid's right about the type of mine. And Rick could have been talking out his ass.*

Yet what other choice did he have?

He could start running out of town immediately, head for the old highway and hope to find help. It would take him an hour to reach the highway, at least, and he had no idea what might be waiting for him there. Certainly not a bomb technician.

Lilly would never last that long. Not even close. She could barely stand on her own now. How could he expect her to stand motionless for hours or even days?

His other option was to hope and pray that someone would just happen to come along, someone with the appropriate knowledge to help, or that the U.N. would hurry back for him.

Stephen knew what hopes and prayers got you in this wasteland. He could hope and pray until the end of time and they might still be standing here when the universe imploded upon itself.

The media liaisons hadn't even bothered to do the head count like they were supposed to before taking off, so his absence might not be noticed until tonight. And even then, who would guess he had been left behind?

More likely, they'd assume he had flaked out like so many journalists before him when they faced the horrors of this war. Some of his colleagues might check for him in the hotel bar, if they checked anywhere.

It could be days before they understood something terrible had happened and even then they might not guess he had been left behind on this trip. Kidnappings and murders were so common in this country, they'd probably assume he was dead in a ditch somewhere and wait for his headless body to arrive in the morgue.

Stephen thought of his wife and daughter and his life back home. Rebecca and Tracy, waiting for him. Desperate for him to return safely. He thought of everything he could lose by making the wrong decision, right here, right now.

What if Rick had been mistaken about the way the Bouncing Betties worked, about that three second delay? Those all-important three seconds. What if the little girl's father had been wrong about the type of mine? What if she was just confused? What if she was right, but he simply wasn't fast enough? What the hell was Stephen doing here anyway?

The little girl whispered, "I'm falling."

"Lilly, you need to stay steady for a little longer, okay? Can you support yourself for a minute?"

She wiped her eyes and nodded. Stephen released her arms, stood and stretched his legs, which were already stiff from kneeling.

She whispered, "Please don't leave me."

"I have to check something over there," Stephen said, pointing at the crumbling remains of a barbershop on the other side of the street. He didn't actually need to check

# AN INSTANT ETERNITY

anything at the barbershop, but he needed to know if he had enough room to implement his insane idea.

"What about me?"

"Stay very still. Everything will be okay," he said, flashing a forced smile. "Don't move. I'll be right back."

She nodded, but Stephen could see how weak she was. Standing like that in the hot sun for even ten minutes had to be tough on her. She obviously hadn't eaten a decent meal in months and the water she'd been drinking was most likely killing her.

Stephen carefully made his way across the street to the ruined barbershop. He avoided any patches of dirt and pavement that seemed suspect and he reached his destination without incident. He stretched his legs again, squatting down, standing back up on his tippy toes, all the time watching the little girl.

The stretches came naturally enough. He had loosened these muscles thousands of times before high school track and field meets, although he had never imagined his legs could ever feel as old and heavy as they did today.

Stephen knew his timing had to be perfect, everything had to be perfect for this crazy idea of his to work, but there also wasn't much time left. He watched the little girl as his mind spun with a million reasons why he should hurry in the opposite direction instead of risking his life.

Lilly was frozen with fear, her eyes locked on him. Her legs were trembling badly and her arms twitched. She was about to lose her balance again, to pass out from the heat and the dehydration, and the mine would kill her where she landed.

Lilly opened her mouth but no sounds emerged. She stared straight at Stephen, her eyes pleading for him to help her, to please do something or she would fall and she knew what that meant and she didn't want to die like her mother. Her eyes bulged and started to roll back into her head.

Before Stephen could have a second thought, before he could say a prayer or think of Rebecca and Tracy and have a change of heart, his legs were moving. He deftly dodged the dirt patches, his shoes hitting the same places he had paced out on his way across the street.

Lilly's swaying became more pronounced and her feet were on the verge of shifting when Stephen grabbed her under her arms and lifted her off the ground.

In the same instant he bent his legs and his knees coiled like springs and he launched himself into the air toward the back of the pick-up truck, pulling Lilly tight to his chest.

Stephen's legs clipped the side of the truck and he tumbled forward, landing on top of Lilly inside the truck bed.

His life flashed before his eyes and Stephen waited for what felt like an eternity for the explosion. Again and again his mind repeated the memory of his father talking about death. Right now, here on this abandoned small town street, he understood his father had been correct: death was making a decision and no mortal could change the outcome one way or another. Death could claim whomever it wanted. There were no exceptions.

Then time snapped back to normal. The three seconds were long past and there had been no explosion. The ragged photographer and the little girl were still alive.

# AN INSTANT ETERNITY

Stephen rolled onto his side and checked Lilly to make sure she hadn't been injured when they landed. The little girl lay there, stunned, her eyes blinking out of sync. Her dirty legs and arms were scraped and dotted with blood, but she was alive.

Stephen gasped in a breath, pushed himself to his knees, and tumbled over the far side of the truck, landing hard on the sidewalk.

He stumbled to his feet, reached back into the bed of the truck, and lifted Lilly up into his arms. He carried her to the town square as quickly as he could, not daring to even glance over his shoulder. He didn't stop until he had passed the war monument.

By then Stephen's entire body was trembling, on the verge of collapsing as the adrenaline rush came to a sudden halt, and he placed Lilly on the bench next to his camera. He leaned against the base of the tall metal soldier and stared down the street. He located the metal prongs of the device in the dirt patch Lilly had been standing on.

*A dud! The damn thing was a dud!* Stephen thought just before the mine was propelled into the air and exploded.

The pick-up truck roared as it flipped into the air. Shrapnel rocketed through the town square, coming so close to Stephen's head that he could feel the superheated metal passing by his ears like a sudden breeze. The sound of the explosion echoed across the valley.

"Jesus," he whispered. His legs lost all their strength and he fell into the tall grasses. They pricked at his exposed skin like tiny knives, but he didn't notice. He didn't care. He couldn't believe he was still alive.

"Are we safe?" the little girl asked, one arm covering her eyes from the beating rays of the sun, the other arm hanging limply off the edge of the bench.

"We made it, Rebecca, we made it," Stephen said, rolling over and staring up at the monument of the soldier, which partially blocked the angry gaze of the summer sun. That tiny bit of shade was a relief. Stephen reached out and took the little girl's hand into his own again.

"Who's Rebecca?"

Stephen realized what he had said. "She's my daughter."

He pushed himself to his feet, his entire body aching from the movement. He felt like he was a million years old. He retrieved his camera, securing it around his neck. He paused for a moment, glanced back at the burning truck, and then he reached into his pocket for the silver chain he had found earlier.

If he hadn't stopped to pick up the necklace, Lilly would have been left standing on the mine all alone until her legs gave out and she died. It was a miracle she was alive. Hell, it was a miracle that *he* was alive.

In that moment of eternity, death had given them a pass. For whatever reason, death hadn't claimed them.

"What's that?" Lilly asked.

"Something to keep you safe," Stephen replied as he put the chain around her neck.

"Thank you," she whispered, her eyes blinking closed. Almost instantly she was sound asleep.

Stephen could understand why. He was exhausted and the heat was nearly enough to knock him back to the ground, but there was no time to waste.

# AN INSTANT ETERNITY

He wrapped his arms under the little girl and he carried her away from the death and the destruction that was her hometown.

He had already decided he would make his way to the old highway and from there they would search for someone with a radio. It was their best and only option, which made the decision easy enough.

While he walked, Stephen thought about his wife and daughter waiting for him in his hometown on the other side of the ocean. The sweltering heat made his muscles twinge and his head spin. His mind bounced from thought to thought.

He didn't want to consider the long road awaiting the little girl. Her journey was just beginning and she had no family, no community. She was trapped in a homeland torn apart by war.

But right now none of that mattered. The little girl needed doctors, she needed medicine, she needed clean water and a safe place to sleep. If she didn't get medical treatment soon, her lack of family and a stable homeland wouldn't be much of a problem for her.

Stephen would shepherd the little girl to safety and then he'd secure a seat on the first flight home to be with his family, even if it meant quitting his job to depart early. He had to flee this cursed land for the sake of his sanity. He desperately hoped he could leave his haunted memories among the overgrown fields and burned towns and rivers full of bloody debris.

Death had given him a second chance and he didn't intend to waste it.

## BRIAN JAMES FREEMAN

Yet for the rest of his life, whenever Stephen closed his eyes, he would see the little girl standing under the hot afternoon sun in the middle of the street, all alone in the abandoned town on the hill overlooking the nuclear power plant. He would never forget Lilly standing in her tattered white dress, frozen in place, her eyes wide and pleading for his help.

That image would haunt Stephen until the end of his natural life, until the moment when eternity returned to claim what it was owed.

# IN THE ROOM

*Bentley Little*

"*In the room, I do my dance.*"
The words, whispered, were told to me in my sleep, by my father.

The next morning he was gone.

—⚏—

I was ten years old when my father abandoned us. He didn't tell anyone he was going, didn't call afterward, didn't even send us a letter. We just woke up one morning, and he was no longer there. We had no idea at first whether he had been killed or kidnapped, whether aliens had abducted him or he'd been taken into the witness protection program. But when Mom told us that he'd packed his clothes and his favorite CDs, when she found out a day or two later that he'd withdrawn money from the bank account (though not all of it), when she learned that he had quit his job *and* given two weeks' notice—in other words, when she realized that he had *planned* this—she sat us down and said simply, in her no-nonsense way, "Your father has abandoned his family."

She never spoke of him again, and if either Clara or I mentioned him, she would immediately change the subject.

Despite the bitter hatred she obviously felt for our father, Mom allowed my sister and me to each keep a picture of him in our respective rooms. There were no other pictures of him in the house—every photo of my parents as a couple had been taken down and put away—but I had one on my dresser of my dad hoisting me on his shoulders in front of the Matterhorn at Disneyland. I was about five in the shot. Clara had a framed photo on her wall of Dad helping her build a sand castle on the beach. I don't know about Clara, because we never talked about it, but as the years passed, I began to forget little things about my father: the type of shoes he wore, his laugh, his favorite food. The picture of him in my mind was missing pieces, no longer complete.

The only thing that remained sharp in my memory was the last thing he said to me, those words, whispered at night, that I had incorporated into a dream: *"In the room, I do my dance."*

---

I was a junior in high school when Liz Nguyen asked me to the Sadie Hawkins dance. I had a crush on her, and I was pretty sure she liked me, too, but the invitation finally confirmed it. The only problem was that I didn't know

# IN THE ROOM

how to dance. I was embarrassed to admit my inadequacy, but I thought it better to come clean, and I told Liz, giving her the chance to back out.

She laughed. "You think I'm some great dancer? I'm not clubbing every night, either. I mean, look at me."

I did. True, she wasn't the type of tight-jeaned, topheavy party girl who was out dancing instead of studying, but from my perspective, she was wonderful. Slender, pretty, bookish but not nerdy, I found her much more attractive than any other girl in my class.

Still, she obviously knew *how* to dance. At least a little bit.

I did not.

I told her that, and she laughed again. She seemed to find my awkwardness endearing rather than embarrassing. "I'll help you," she said. "We can practice in my bedroom."

*"In the room, I do my dance."*

The thought gave me a slight chill, and I shivered. "Do you…often practice dancing in your room?" I asked.

"Oh sure," she said. "That way I can watch myself in the mirror and see how I look. So I can correct anything I'm doing wrong," she added quickly. "Not to, you know, *admire* myself or anything."

I smiled.

"I'm serious!" she hit my shoulder.

"Okay," I agreed. "We can practice."

Despite her modesty, Liz was actually quite a good dancer, and for the next week, we spent at least an hour every afternoon going over some simple steps. Despite my clumsiness, she was able to teach me a slow dance where I basically lurched from side to side, holding her hands, and a slightly quicker dance for fast songs where I stood in place, arms cocked at my sides, and sort of...exercised.

The following week, the week before the dance, we saw each other briefly in the halls and talked on the phone a few times, but we both had midterm tests and a lot of homework, so we didn't get to practice, though I did it myself in front of my own mirror and thought I didn't look too bad. At least, I didn't think I'd embarrass myself.

Sadie Hawkins Day was a Friday, and the dance was that evening in the gym. In keeping with tradition, *she* would be the one to pick *me* up. She'd also bought the tickets for the event and came with a boutonniere that she pinned to my shirt. Without the pretext of dance practice, we were forced to have an actual conversation, and on the drive over, I flailed about, unsuccessfully trying to come up with a conversation topic that would last more than a few sentences. Liz wasn't much better at the small talk, but there was something self-possessed about her, an inner stillness that I hadn't seen before and that made me feel like a bumbling oaf. I hadn't talked to her for a few days, and out of desperation, I asked, "What did you do yesterday?" I knew she'd probably just gone to school and then gone home, as I had, and I was trying to come up with a followup question when she answered me.

"In the room," she said, "I do my dance."

I froze. It was the same thing my father had said all those years ago, and my heart started pounding at the words.

But we had arrived at the school parking lot and there was no time to discuss what she had told me. I was not even sure I *wanted* to discuss it. I was a little bit afraid of her now and was grateful when we got out of the car

# IN THE ROOM

and I saw my friend Devon getting out of Sheri Stillman's Accord. Holding Liz's hand, I hurried over to say hi, and all four of us walked into the gym together.

Standing next to Devon, I watched Liz as she and Sharon went to get us punch.

*"In the room, I do my dance."*

There was something different in the way she walked, that same self-possession I'd noticed earlier, and I could not help feeling that the Liz Nguyen here tonight was not the same one who had invited me to the dance two weeks ago.

We drank punch, we mingled, but eventually I knew we were going to have to go out onto the floor, and when the DJ put on one of the songs we had practiced to, Liz took my hand and led me into the fray.

She danced differently than she had in her room, and I could not keep up. I thought she might tone it down a little to stay at my level, but she didn't, and after two songs I backed off and went over to the drinks table, leaving her to dance alone. She was the only one not paired up with a date, and as I watched from afar, I saw that there was something unhinged about her movements, something crazy. I was not the only one to notice it. Others did, too, and gradually the dance floor cleared as students grew uncomfortable around her and moved away.

The thought of being alone with her in the car on the way home gave me a sinking feeling in the pit of my stomach, and I asked Devon if he and Sheri could give me a ride and drop me off at home before they went wherever they were going to go to park.

"Shouldn't you tell Liz?" Devon asked, nodding toward where she was twirling in the center of the gym.

"No," I said. "I don't think so."

Liz was not at school on Monday, and when I called her house that night to find out if she was sick, I got her mom on the phone, who burst into tears at the mention of her name and hung up on me.

She never came back to school, though her name continued to be called at roll in the Social Studies class we had together, and no one I knew ever saw her again.

—⚘—

I graduated from college with a degree in English. I wanted to be a writer, but knew I had to have a day job to fall back on, and I obtained a teaching job at a charter school in Anaheim Hills. The teaching went better than the writing, and by my second summer as an instructor I had given up even pretending to write the novel that I'd told everyone I was working on. I spent my two-and-a-half months off going to movies, going to the beach, hanging out with friends. I spent the Fourth of July weekend with my mom and sister.

In late August, I was at a school supply store, looking for some new posters to hang on my classroom bulletin boards during the coming year, when I saw through the front window a woman in the parking lot outside waving at someone inside the store. I didn't recognize her and assumed she was waving at someone else, but when I bought my posters and walked outside, heading across the lot toward my car, the woman approached me. She was nondescript, in her late forties or early fifties, dressed plainly in brown, but there was an expression of purpose

# IN THE ROOM

on her face that made me quicken my step. I didn't know if she was going to harangue me about some cause or ask me for money, but I could tell that she wanted to talk to me, and my goal was to get in the car before she reached me.

I didn't make it.

Our paths intersected some five feet from my trunk, and she stopped and stood there, facing me. "Can I help you?" I asked.

"In the room," she said softly, "you can write your story."

Her words chilled me to the bone.

*In the room...*

"What are you talking about?" I said, trying to sound bolder than I felt. There were goosebumps on my arms.

She grabbed my hand, turned it palm up, and before I could pull it away, she was writing on it with a black marker that I had not noticed she was holding. She was finished in seconds and immediately started walking away.

"Hey!" I called, but she didn't turn around, and I didn't really want her to.

I looked down at my palm, turning it around so I could see what she'd written. As I'd feared, as I'd somehow known, it was an address.

*In the room...*

How had she known I wanted to be a writer? Was "the room" she mentioned related to the one my dad had told me about? There were too many questions and none of them had answers.

The address on my hand was not nearby. I lived in Anaheim, and the street whose name she'd written down was somewhere in Los Angeles. I'd heard it mentioned on newscasts—probably in connection with crimes of some sort. I knew I was going to go there and check it out, and rather than go back home and think things over and try to come to a logical decision, I decided to just head straight there. I filled up with gas at a nearby Arco station, plugged in my GPS and got on the Santa Ana Freeway, heading west.

The address turned out to be downtown, amidst the high rise buildings in the center of the city. I'd had no idea what to expect and on the way over had imagined everything from a warehouse to a mansion to a fleabag hotel. But it was one of those original Los Angeles high rises, a concrete office building with identical rows of small windows, the kind that was often shown in black-and-white movies from the 1940s. It was smaller than the steel-and-glass monstrosities flanking it, but it was still a tall building, and though it was old, it was still in use, and I saw people walking in and out of the glass front doors as I passed by.

It took me a couple of tours around several blocks and down several confusing one-way streets before I finally found a parking spot in front of a closed Italian restaurant. I had no quarters for the meter, but it was one of those new devices that took credit cards, so I charged an hour's worth of time and walked back down a side street to the building.

At the gas station, I'd copied the information off my hand onto the front of an Auto Club map of California that I kept in the glove compartment, just in case the ink sweated off my palm as I drove. But the information was still visible on my skin, and I walked inside the building's

# IN THE ROOM

lobby, then looked at the room number: 511. Fifth floor, I assumed, and I headed over to the bank of elevators and took the first one up.

The fifth floor corridor was empty, but I heard music coming from down the hall, and I followed the sound. Sure enough, it was coming from behind the last door on the floor, a wooden door with peeling paint that looked as though it belonged in a tenement apartment building. At eye level three metal numerals had been nailed to the wood: 511.

There was no bell, so I knocked, and when no one responded, I knocked again. I heard other noises in addition to the music, noises I could not identify, but no one opened the door, so I reached out, tried the knob and turned it.

The room before me was dim, if not dark, and there were no windows or lights that I could see. Much larger than I expected, it was crowded and busy, filled with people. One of them was a man in a smock painting an abstract picture on a gigantic canvas. One of them was a woman playing a piano.

One of them was my dad.

And he was dancing.

I stood there, just inside the doorway, rooted in place. He had not changed one iota in all the years that had passed. His hair was the same, there were no lines on his face, he even appeared to be wearing the same clothes. Leaping into the air and twisting around, he saw me.

"I knew you would come!" he shouted, and there was joy in his voice.

It frightened me to see him. Not only because he had not aged, but because of the *way* he danced, the movements themselves. There was a reckless abandon in his flailing arms and legs, a chaotic freedom that I had never associated with my father. Only it was more than that. The movements were *wrong*. He danced in a manner that people were not supposed to dance, a spontaneous and horrifying choreography that should not have existed and that frightened me to the core of my being.

Liz Nguyen was there, too, I saw now, and she, too, was performing a terrifying routine that went against nature and everything I believed in. My reaction made no sense—it was only a dance, after all—but it was what I felt and it was true. This was an extreme extension of what she'd been doing the last time I saw her, when she cleared the gym floor of all other students. It was a profane and hateful dance she was performing, and though she was smiling, there was something terrible in that smile. Like my father, she had not aged, and she was the same 17-year-old I had left at the Sadie Hawkins Dance nearly a decade ago.

I waited for my dad to say something else to me. We hadn't seen each other since I was ten, and surely he wanted to apologize or tell me how much he missed me and loved me or…something.

But he did not.

He continued with his horrible endless dance, and he was no longer even looking in my direction.

How long had he been doing this? Decades? When he spoke those final words to me—

*In the room, I do my dance*

# IN THE ROOM

—he sounded as though he had danced here before. But how often and for how long? And what about since he'd left us? He hadn't aged at all. Was this all he did? Did he ever stop? Did he ever have to sleep? Did he even eat?

He was still dancing, and the sight was maddening, infuriating. I wanted him to stop. I wanted him to acknowledge my presence. I wanted him to hug me or shake my hand or at least *stop dancing*.

But he would not, and I wished he would trip and fall and *have* to stop. Or, better still, have a heart attack and collapse to the floor, clutching his chest.

I wanted him dead.

Liz Nguyen was still doing her own dance, and the other individuals in the room were painting their pictures or playing their music or making their speeches or doing whatever it was that they did.

The nondescript woman who'd written the address on my palm was next to me, though I didn't know where she'd come from. "In the room," she whispered, "you can kill your father."

My dad continued to dance. He hadn't said a word to me since that initial greeting, and I hated him for it. I noticed for the first time that there was what looked like a lance leaning against the wall to my right.

*In the room, you can kill your father.*

I didn't plan on killing him. I just wanted to get his attention. I just wanted him to *stop*. But when I picked up the lance, intending only to trip him and put an end to that exasperating dance, I swung it hard, like a baseball bat, at his legs. Seconds before, my goal had been merely to get him to halt, but now I wanted to *break* his legs, and

I thrilled to the satisfying impact that jolted my arms as I brought him down. He fell, sprawling on the dirty wooden floor, and before he could get up again, I lifted the lance high and smashed it into his legs as hard as I could. I did it again and again, and then I moved up to his arms and then his head and then he was dead.

No one noticed, no one cared. The painter kept painting, Liz kept dancing, everyone continued doing what they were doing as though nothing had happened.

Sweating, breathing hard, I dropped the lance on the floor.

The woman from the parking lot was still standing next to me. She pointed toward a desk against the far wall, barely visible in the gloom. "In the room, you can write your story," she repeated.

I ran away. My arms hurt, my chest hurt, my overtaxed lungs could barely suck in enough air to keep me from passing out, but I made it down the hall to the elevators, and I took the first one down and staggered onto the street. Bending over, grabbing my knees, I breathed deeply, trying to calm down. I didn't want to think about what had happened, what I had done, and as quickly as I could, I started down the street and then the side street, to my car.

Back in Orange County, I drove directly to my sister's house, hoping this was her day off, hoping she was home. She was. I had regained my composure on the drive over, and the car's air-conditioning had stopping my sweating, but I was still confused and in turmoil, and Clara sensed that when she saw me.

"What's wrong?" she asked instantly. "What happened?"

# IN THE ROOM

"Dad," I said. "I saw Dad."

"You saw him?" Clara grabbed my shoulders. "Where was it? What did he look like? Did you ask him why he left? Why he never even called or sent us a card?"

I didn't know what to tell her, didn't know what to say.

"Did you talk to him? What was he doing?"

I took a deep breath.

"In the room," I said, "he did his dance."

# FLYING SOLO

### Ed Gorman

*(He went with her to every appointment. Never missed. Diagnosis. Surgery. Chemo. Radiation. When the oncologist gave her the great news—"We're calling this a complete success, Ruth"—they were off to London for two weeks. Couldn't really afford it but what the hell.)*

"YOU SMOKING AGAIN?"

"Yeah." Ralph's sly smile. "You afraid these'll give me cancer?"

"You mind rolling down the window then?"

"I bought a pack today. It felt good. I've been wanting a cigarette for twenty-six years. That's how long ago I gave them up. I was still walking a beat back then. I figure what the hell, you know. I mean the way things are. I've been debating this a long time. I don't know why I picked today to start again. I just did." He rolled the window down. The soft summer night came in like a sweet angel of mercy.

"I've smoked four of them but this is the only one I've really enjoyed."

"Why this one?"

"Because I got to see your face."

"The Catholic thing?"

"That's right, kid. The Catholic thing. They've got you so tight inside you need an enema. No cheating on the wife, no cheating on the taxes, no cheating on the church. And somebody bends the rules a little, your panties get all bunched up."

"You're pretty eloquent for an ex-cop. That enema remark. And also, by the way, whenever you call me 'kid' people look at you funny. I mean I'm sixty-six and you're sixty-eight."

Ralph always portrayed himself as a swashbuckler; the day he left the force he did so with seventeen citizen complaints on his record.

He took a long, deep drag on his Winston. "We're upping the ante tonight, Tom. That's why I'm a little prickish. I know you hate being called 'kid.' It's just nerves."

I was surprised he admitted something like that. He enjoyed playing fearless.

"That waitress didn't have it coming, Ralph."

"How many times you gonna bring that up? And for the record, I did ask for a cheeseburger if you'll remember and I did leave her a frigging ten-dollar tip after I apologized to her twice. See how uptight you are?"

"She probably makes six bucks an hour and has a kid at home."

"You're just a little bit nervous the way I am. That's why you're runnin' your mouth so hard."

# FLYING SOLO

He was probably right. "So we're really going to do it, huh?"

"Yeah, Tom, we're really going to do it."

"What time is it?"

I checked my Timex, the one I got when I retired from teaching high school for twenty-six years. English and creative writing. The other gift I got was not being assaulted by any of my students. A couple of my friends on the staff had been beaten, one of them still limping years after. "Nine minutes later than when you asked me last time."

"By rights I should go back of that tree over there and take a piss. In fact I think I will."

"That's just when he'll pull in."

"The hell with it. I wouldn't be any good with a full bladder."

"You won't be any good if he sees us."

"He'll be so drunk he won't notice." The grin made him thirty. "You worry too much."

The moon told its usual lies. Made this ugly two-story flat-roofed cube of a house if not beautiful at least tolerable to the quick and forgiving eye. The steep sagging stairs running at a forty-five degree angle up the side of the place was all that interested me. That and the isolation here on the edge of town. A farmhouse at one time, a tumbledown barn behind it, the farmland back to seed, no one here except our couple living in the upstairs. Ken and Callie Neely. Ken being the one we were after.

We were parked behind a stretch of oaks. Easy to watch him pull in and start up those stairs. I kept the radio low. Springsteen.

When Ralph got back in I handed him my pocket-sized hand sanitizer.

"You shoulda been a den mother."

"You take a piss, you wash your hands."

"Yes, Mom."

And then we heard him. He drove his sleek red Chevy pickup truck so fast he sounded as if he was going to shoot right on by. I wondered what the night birds silver-limned in the broken moonlight of the trees made of the country-western song bellering from the truck. A breeze swooped in the open windows of my Volvo and brought the scents of long-dead summers. *An image of a seventeen-year-old girl pulling her T-shirt over her head and the immortal perfection of her pink-tipped breasts.*

"You know what this is going to make us, don't you? I mean after we've done it."

"Yeah, I do, Tom. It's gonna make us happy. That's what it's gonna make us. Now let's go get him."

—⚍—

*(Six month check-up three years later. Nurse calls and says Doctor would like her to come in and talk about the results. "Stage Four." She handles it better than he does. He secretly starts seeing a psychologist. Needs to be strong for her. But the terror is overwhelming him. Help me.)*

I met Ralph Francis McKenna in the chemo room of Oncology Partners. His was prostate, mine was colon. They gave him a year, me eighteen months, no guarantees either of us would make it. We had one other thing in common.

# FLYING SOLO

We were both widowers. Our kids lived way across the country and could visit only occasionally. Natural enough we'd become friends. Of a kind, anyway.

We always arranged to have our chemo on the same day, same time. After the chemo was over we both had to take monthly IVs of other less powerful drugs.

Ralph said he'd had the same reaction when he'd first walked into the huge room where thirty-eight patients sat in comfortable recliners getting various kinds of IV drips. So many people smiling and laughing. Another thing being how friendly everybody was to everybody else. People in thousand-dollar coats and jackets talking to threadbare folks in cheap discount clothes. Black people yukking it up with white people. And swift efficient nurses Ralph Francis McKenna, a skilled flirt, knew how to draw in.

Once in awhile somebody would have a reaction to the chemo. One woman must have set some kind of record for puking. She was so sick the three nurses hovering over her didn't even have time to get her to one of the johns. All they could do was keep shoving clean pans under her chin.

During our third session Ralph said, "So how do you like flying solo?"

"What's 'flying solo'?"

"You know. Being alone. Without a wife."

"I hate it. My wife knew how to enjoy life. She really loved it. I get depressed a lot. I should've gone first. She appreciated being alive."

"I still talk to my wife, you know that? I walk around the house and talk to her like we're just having a conversation."

"I do pretty much the same thing. One night I dreamed I was talking to her on the phone and when I woke up I was sitting on the side of the bed with the receiver in my hand."

Flying solo. I liked that phrase.

You could read, use one of their DVD players or listen to music on headsets. Or visit with friends and relatives who came to pass the time. Or in Ralph's case, flirt.

The nurses liked him. His good looks and cop self-confidence put them at ease. I'm sure a couple of the single ones in their forties would probably have considered going to bed with him if he'd been capable of it. He joked to me once, shame shining in his eyes: "They took my pecker, Tom, and they won't give it back." Not that a few of the older nurses didn't like me. There was Nora who reminded me of my wife in her younger years. A few times I started to ask her out but then got too scared. The last woman I'd asked out on a first date had been my wife forty-three years ago.

The DVD players were small and you could set them up on a wheeled table right in front of your recliner while you were getting the juice. One day I brought season two of *The Rockford Files* with James Garner. When I got about two minutes into the episode I heard Ralph sort of snicker.

"What's so funny?"

"You. I should've figured you for a Garner type of guy."

"What's wrong with Garner?"

"He's a wuss. Sort of femmy."

# FLYING SOLO

"James Garner is sort of femmy?"

"Yeah. He's always whining and bitching. You know, like a woman. I'm more of a Clint Eastwood fan myself."

"I should've figured on that."

"You don't like Eastwood?"

"Maybe I would if he knew how to act."

"He's all man."

"He's all something all right."

"You never hear him whine."

"That's because he doesn't know how. It's too complicated for him."

"'Make my day.'"

"Kiss my ass."

Ralph laughed so hard several of the nurses down the line looked at us and smiled. Then they tried to explain us to their patients.

---

*(Chemo dosage is so strong she loses fifteen pounds—and was thin already—and the docs are very concerned about the vomiting and the diarrhea. Both sons and their families visit. Ted, the youngest, collapses into his father's arms, sobbing.)*

A nurse named Heather Moore was the first one. She always called us her "Trouble Boys" because we kidded her so much about her somewhat earnest, naïve worldview. Over a couple of months, we learned that her ex-husband had wiped out their tiny bank account and run off with the secretary at the muffler shop where he'd been manager. She always said, "All my girlfriends say I should be a whole lot madder at him but you know when I'm honest with myself I probably wasn't that good of a wife. You know? His mom always fixed these big suppers for the family. And she's a very pretty woman. But by the time I put in eight hours here and pick up Bobby at daycare, I just don't have much energy. We ate a lot of frozen stuff. And I put on about ten pounds extra. I guess you can't blame him for looking around."

Couple times after she started sharing her stories with us, Ralph made some phone calls. He talked to three people who'd known her husband. A chaser who'd started running around on Heather soon after their wedding day. A slacker at work and a husband who betrayed his wife in maybe the worst way of all—making constant jokes about her to his coworkers. And she blamed herself for not being good enough for him.

Then came the day when she told us about the duplex where she lived. The toilets wouldn't flush properly, the garbage disposal didn't work, both front and back concrete steps were dangerously shattered and the back door wouldn't lock. Some of her neighbors had been robbed recently.

The landlord was a jerk—lawyer, of course—named David Muldoon. Despite the comic book surname he was anything but comic. Ralph checked him out. A neo-yuppie who owned several income properties in the city, he was apparently working his way up the slumlord ladder. Heather complained to the city and the city did what it did best, nothing. She'd called Muldoon's business office several times and been promised that her complaints would soon be taken care of. They weren't. And even baby lawyers fresh from the diploma mills wanted more than she could afford to take Muldoon on.

We always asked her how it was going with Muldoon. The day she told us that the roof was leaking and nobody from his office had returned her call in four days, Ralph told her, "You don't worry about it anymore, Heather."

"How come?"

"I just have a feeling."

Heather wasn't the only one wondering what the hell he was talking about. So was I. He said, "You got the usual big night planned?"

"If you mean frozen dinner, some TV, maybe calling one of my kids who'll be too busy to talk very long and then going to bed, yes."

"Maybe watch a little James Garner?"

"Yeah or put on Clint Eastwood and fall asleep early."

"Glad you don't have plans because we're going on a stakeout."

"I go to bed at nine."

"Not tonight. Unless we get lucky. Maybe he'll get laid and get home before then."

"Who?"

"Muldoon, that's who."

"You know for a fact that he's got something going on the side?"

"No. But I always listen to my gut."

I smiled.

"I say something funny?" Sort of pissed the way he said it.

"Do all you guys watch bad cop shows before you graduate? Your 'gut'?"

"Most of these assholes cheat."

I thought about it. "Maybe you're right."

"Kid, I'm always right." Grin this time.

Turned out it was the secretary in the law firm on the floor below Muldoon's. Not even all that attractive. He was just out for strange in the nighttime.

We waited leaning against his new black Cadillac.

"Who the fuck are you two supposed to be?"

"We're supposed to be the two guys you least want to hear from." I was happy to let Ralph do the talking.

"Yeah?" All swagger.

"Yeah. You're taking advantage of a friend of ours."

"Get the fuck out of my way. I'm going home."

"It's a bitch getting rid of that pussy smell on your clothes, isn't it? Wives like to pretend they can't smell it."

Dug out his cell phone. Waggled it for us. "I don't know who you two assholes are but I'll bet the police won't have any trouble finding out."

"And your wife won't have any trouble finding out about the snatch in that apartment house behind us, either."

I didn't realize what had happened until I saw the counselor bend in half and heard him try to swear while his lungs were collapsing. He fell to his knees. Ralph hit him so hard on the side of the head Muldoon toppled over. "Her name's Heather Moore. She's one of your tenants. She doesn't know anything about this so don't bother trying to shake her down for any information. You've got two days to fix everything wrong in her apartment. Two days or I

# FLYING SOLO

call your wife. And if you come after us or send anybody after us then I not only call your wife I start looking for any other bimbos you've been with in the past. I'm a retired homicide detective so I know how to do this shit. You got me?"

Muldoon still couldn't talk. Just kept rolling back and forth on the sandy concrete. He grunted something.

—⚋—

*(He wants one good long visit with her before she passes but it is not to be. The sickness seizes her completely and she turns inward, alone in the darkness of her own death. There are smiles sometimes, even a weak joke or two when she can summon a few fleeting moments of strength. An hour before she is pronounced dead in the hospice he sits next to her bed holding her hand. He won't let go of her until the doctor gently insists.)*

That was how it started. Heather asked us about it once but we said we didn't know anything about it. Heather obviously didn't believe us because two weeks later a nurse named Sally Coates, one neither of us knew very well, came and sat down on a chair next to the IV stand and told us about her husband and this used-car salesman who'd sold them a lemon and wouldn't make it right. They were out seven grand they hadn't been able to afford in the first place but they had to have a car so her husband could get to the VA hospital where he was learning to walk again after losing his right leg in Afghanistan. The kind of story you watch on TV and want to start killing people.

All innocence Ralph said, "Gosh, Sally, I wish we could help you but I don't see what we could do. There isn't any reason he'd listen to us."

"I can't believe it," Sally said the next time we saw her. "Bob got a call the day after I told you about this salesman. The guy said to bring the car in and they'd get it fixed up right so we wouldn't be having any trouble with it. And there wouldn't be any charge."

"I'll bet you did a lot of praying about it, didn't you, Sally?"

"Of course. We have two little ones to feed. Keeping that car running was breaking us."

"Well, it was the prayers that did it, Sally."

"And you didn't have anything to do with it?"

"Ask him."

I shook my head. "What could we have done, Sally? We're just two old guys."

After she left, Ralph leaned over from his leather recliner and said, "The only good thing about dying this way is we don't have to give a shit about anything. What're they gonna do to us?" That grin of his. "We're already dead."

I developed a uniform. A Cubs cap, dark aviator glasses and a Louisville Slugger. According to Ralph I was "the backup hood. They're scared enough of me. Then they see this guy with the ball bat and the shades—they'll do anything to cooperate." He didn't mention how old we were.

The nurses kept coming. Four in the next three months. A nurse who was trying to get a collection of family photographs back from an ex-boyfriend she'd broken up with after he'd given her the clap, spurned boyfriend stealing the collection and keeping it for her breaking up with him; the nurse whose daughter's boyfriend was afraid to visit because two bully brothers down the block always picked on him when he pulled up; and the nurse who liked to sit in on poker games with five guys who worked at an electronics discount house and thought it was pretty damned funny to cheat her out of forty to sixty dollars every time she sat down. It took her four months of playing twice a month to figure it out.

No heavy lifting, as they say; no, that came with a tiny, delicate young nurse named Callie. We noticed the bruises on her arms first then the bruises on her throat despite the scarf she wore with her uniform. Then came the two broken fingers and the way she limped for a couple of weeks and finally the faint but unmistakable black eye. A few of the other nurses whispered about it among themselves. One of them told us that the head nurse had asked Callie about it. Callie had smiled and said that "my whole family is clumsy."

It was during this time that both Ralph and I realized that we probably wouldn't be beating the prognoses we'd been given. With me it was a small but certain track of new cancer suddenly appearing on my right thigh; with Ralph it was the return of heart problems he'd had off and on for two decades.

We didn't talk about it much to each other. There isn't much to say when you get to this point. You just hope for as much decent time as you can get and if you've been helping people here and there you go right on helping them as long as you can.

We followed Callie home one night, found out that she lived in a tumbledown farmhouse as isolated as a lighthouse. The next night we followed her home and when she stopped off at a shopping center we waited for her by her car.

She smiled. "My two favorite patients. I guess you don't get to see me enough in chemo, huh?" The cat green eyes were suspicious despite her greeting. She'd developed another one of those mysterious limps.

"That's right. Tom here wants to ask you to marry him."

"Well," the smile never wavering, "maybe I should talk that over with my husband first. You think?"

"That's what we want to talk to you about, Callie," I said. "Your husband."

The smile went and so did she. Or at least she tried. I stood in front of the car door. Ralph took her arm and walked her about four feet away.

He said something to her I couldn't hear but her I heard clearly: "My personal life is none of your damn business! And I'm going to tell my husband about this."

"He going to beat us up the way he beats you up?"

"Who said he beats me up?"

"I was a cop, remember? I've seen dozens of cases like yours. They run to a pattern."

"Well, then you weren't a very *good* cop because my husband has never laid a hand on me."

"Three restraining orders in five years; six 911 calls; the same ER doctor who said he's dealt with you twice for concussions; and a woman's shelter that told me you came there twice for three-night stays."

# FLYING SOLO

The city roared with life—traffic, stray rap music, shouts, laughter, squealing tires—but right here a little death was being died as she was forced to confront not just us but herself. The small package she'd been carrying slipped from her hands to the concrete and she slumped against her car. She seemed to rip the sobs from herself in tiny increments, like somebody in the early stages of a seizure.

"I've tried to get away. Five or six times. One night I took the kids and got all the way to St. Joe. Missouri, I mean. We stayed in a motel there for two weeks. Took every dime I had. The kids didn't mind. They're as scared of him as I am. But he found us. He never told me how. And you know what he did? He was waiting for us when we got back from going to a movie the kids wanted to see. He was in our room. I opened the door and there he was. He looked down at Luke—he's eight now; he was only four then—and he said, 'You take care of your little sister, Luke. You two go sit in my truck now.' 'You better not hurt her, Dad.' Can you imagine that; a four-year-old talking like that? A four-year-old? Anyway then he looked at me and said, 'Get in here, whore.' He waited until I closed the door behind me and then he hit me so hard in the face he broke my nose. And my glasses. He forced the kids to ride back with him. That way he knew I'd come back, too."

This was in the food court of the mall where we'd convinced her to come and have some coffee with us. You could reach up and grab a handful of grease from the air. I'm told in Texas they deep-fry quarter sticks of butter. If it ever comes up here this mall will sell it for sure.

"But you always come back."

"I love him, Ralph. I can't explain it. It's like a sickness."

"It's not 'like' a sickness, Callie. It *is* a sickness."

"Maybe if I knew I could get away and he'd never find me. To him those restraining orders are a joke." Then: "I have to admit there're some times—more and more these days I guess—when I think maybe it'd be best if he'd just get killed driving that damned truck of his. You know, an accident where he's the only one killed. I wouldn't want to do that to anybody else." Then: "Isn't that awful?"

"It is if you love him."

"I say that, Tom. I *always* say that. But the woman at the shelter had me see a counselor and the counselor explained to me what she called the 'dynamics' of how I really feel about him. We had to take two semesters of psych to get our nursing degrees so I'd always considered myself pretty smart on the subject. But she led me into thinking a lot of things that had never occurred to me before. And so even though I say that, I'm not sure I mean it." Then, shy: "Sorry for all the carrying on in the parking lot. I attracted quite a crowd."

"I collected admission from every one of them."

She sat back in her curved red plastic chair and smiled. "You guys; you're really my friends. I was so depressed all day. Even with the kids there I just didn't want to drag myself home tonight. I know I was being selfish to even think such a thing. But I just couldn't take being hit or kicked anymore. I knew he'd be mad that I stopped at the mall. Straight home or I'd better have a damned good excuse. Or I'll be sorry. It's no way to live."

"No," I said, "it sure isn't."

"Now let's go get him."

Callie had mentioned she was taking the kids for a long weekend stay at a theme park which was why we'd decided on tonight.

Neely didn't hear us coming. We walked through patches of shadow then moonlight, shadow then moonlight while he tried to get out of his truck. I say tried because he was so drunk he almost came out headfirst and would have if he hadn't grabbed the edge of the truck door in time. Then he sat turned around on the edge of the seat and puked straight down. He went three times and he made me almost as sick as he was. Then of course being as drunk as he was he stepped down with his cowboy boots into the puddle of puke he'd made. He kept wiping the back of his right hand across his mouth. He started sloshing through the puke then stopped and went back to the truck. He opened the door and grabbed something. In the moonlight I could see it was a pint of whiskey. He gunned a long drink then took six steps and puked it all right back up. He stepped into this puke as well and headed more or less in the direction of the stairs that would take him to his apartment. All of this was setting things up perfectly. Nobody was going to question the fact that Neely had been so drunk it was no surprise that he'd fallen off those stairs and died.

We moved fast. I took the position behind him with my ball cap, shades and ball bat and Ralph got in front of him with his Glock.

Neely must've been toting a 2.8 level of alcohol because he didn't seem to be aware of Ralph until he ran straight into him. And straight into the Glock. Even then all he could say was, "Huh? I jush wan' sleep."

"Good evening, Mr. Neely. You shouldn't drink so much. You need to be alert when you're beating the shit out of women half your size. You never know when they're going to hit back, do you?"

"Hey, dude, ish tha' a gun?"

"Sure looks like it, doesn't it?"

He reeled back on the heels of his cowboy boots. I poked the bat into his back. I was careful. When he went down the stairs it had to look accidental. We couldn't bruise him or use any more force than it took to give him a slight shove. If he didn't die the first time down he would the second time we shoved him.

"Hey."

"You need some sleep, Neely."

"—need no fuckin' sleep. 'n don't try'n make me. Hey, an' you got a fuckin' gun."

"What if I told you that I've got a pizza in the car?"

"Pizza?"

"Yeah. Pizza."

"How come pizza?"

"So we can sit down in your apartment and talk things over."

"Huh?"

"How—does—pizza—sound?"

Ralph was enunciating because Neely was about two minutes away from unconsciousness. We had to get him up those stairs without leaving any marks on him.

# FLYING SOLO

"Pizza, Neely. Sausage and beef and pepperoni."

I allowed myself the pleasure of taking in the summer night. The first time I'd ever made love to Karen had been on a night like this near a boat dock. Summer of our senior year in college. We went back to that spot many times over the years. Not long before she died we went there, too. I almost believed in ghosts; I thought I saw our younger selves out on the night river in one of those old rented aluminum canoes, our lives all ahead of us, so young and exuberant and naïve. I wanted to get in one of those old canoes and take my wife down river so she could die in my arms and maybe I'd be lucky and die in hers as well. But it hadn't worked out that way. All too soon I'd been flying solo.

Neely started puking again. This time it was a lot more dramatic because after he finished he fell facedown in it.

"This fucking asshole. When he's done you take one arm and I'll take the other one."

"I thought we weren't going to touch him."

"That's why you shoved those latex gloves in your back pocket same as I did. You gotta plan for contingencies. That's why cops carry guns they can plant on perps. Otherwise we'll be here all night. Clint Eastwood would know about that."

"Yes, planting guns on people. Another admirable Eastwood quality."

"Right. I forgot. Tender ears. You don't want to hear about real life. You just want to bitch and moan like Garner. Now let's pick up this vile piece of shit and get it over with."

He'd worked up a pretty good sweat with all his puking. It was a hot and humid night. His body was soggy like something that would soon mildew. Once I pulled him out of his puke I held my breath.

"We don't want to drag him. They'll look at his boots. Stand him upright and we'll sort of escort him to the steps."

"I just hope he doesn't start puking again."

"I saw a black perp puke like this once. I wish I had it on tape."

"Yeah, be fun for the grandkids to watch at Christmastime."

"I like that, Tom. Smart-ass remarks in the course of committing murder one. Shows you're getting a lot tougher."

We took our time. He didn't puke again but from the tangy odor I think he did piss his pants.

When we were close to the bottom step, he broke. I guess both of us had assumed he was unconscious and therefore wouldn't be any problem. But he broke and he got a three or four second lead while we just stood there and watched him scramble up those stairs like a wild animal that had just escaped its cage. He was five steps ahead of us before Ralph started after him. I pounded up the steps right behind him. Ralph was shouting. I'm sure he had to restrain himself from just shooting Neely and getting it over with.

Neely was conscious enough to run but not conscious enough to think clearly because when he got to the top of the stairs he stopped and dug a set of keys from his pocket. As he leaned in to try and find the lock his head jerked up suddenly and he stared at us as if he was seeing us for the very first time. Confusion turned to terror in his eyes and he started backing away from us. "Hey, who the hell're you?"

"Who do you think we are, Neely?"

"I don' like thish."

"Yeah, well we don't like it, either."

"He got a ball bat." He nodded in my direction. He weaved wide as he did so, so wide I thought he was going to tip over sideways. Then his hand searched the right pocket of his Levi's. It looked like he'd trapped an angry ferret in there.

Ralph materialized Neely's nine-inch switchblade. "This what you're looking for?"

"Hey," Neely said. And when he went to grab for it he started falling to the floor. Ralph grabbed him in time. Stood him straight up.

But Neely wasn't done yet. And he was able to move faster than I would have given him credit for. Ralph glanced back at me, nodded for me to come forward. And in that second Neely made his sloppy, drunken move. He grabbed the switchblade from Ralph's hand and immediately went into a crouch.

He would have been more impressive if he hadn't swayed side to side so often. And if he hadn't tried to sound tough. "Who'sh gotta knife now, huh?"

"You gonna cut us up are you, Neely?"

All the time advancing on Neely, backing him up. "C'mon, Neely. Cut me. Right here." Ralph held his arm out. "Right there, Neely. You can't miss it."

Neely swaying, half-stumbling backward as Ralph moved closer, closer. "You're pretty pathetic, you know that Neely? You beat up your wife all the time and even when you've got the knife you're still scared of me. You're not much of a man but then you know that, don't you? You look in the mirror every morning and you see yourself for what you really are, don't you?"

I doubt Neely understood what Ralph was saying to him. This was complex stuff to comprehend when you were as wasted as Neely was. All he seemed to understand was that Ralph meant to do him harm. And if Ralph didn't do it there was always the guy in the ball cap and the shades. You know, with the bat.

Neely stumbled backward, his arms circling in a desperate attempt to keep himself upright. He hit the two-by-four that was the upper part of the porch enclosure just at the lower part of his back and he went right over, the two-by-four splintering as he did so. He didn't scream. My guess is he was still confused about what was happening. By the time he hit the ground I was standing next to Ralph, looking down into the shadows beneath us.

There was silence. Ralph got his flashlight going and we got our first look at him. If he wasn't dead he was pretty good at faking it. He didn't land in any of those positions we associate with people who died crashing from great heights. He was flat on his back with his arms flung wide. His right leg was twisted inward a few inches but nothing dramatic. The eyes were open and looked straight up. No expression of horror, something else we've picked up from books and movies. And as we watched the blood started pooling from the back of his head.

"Let's go make sure," Ralph said.

# FLYING SOLO

It was like somebody had turned on the soundtrack. In the moments it had taken Neely to fall all other sound had disappeared. But now the night was back and turned up high. Night birds, dogs, horses and cows bedded down for the evening, distant trucks and trains all turned so high I wanted to clap my hands to my ears.

"You all right, Tom?"

"Why wouldn't I be all right?"

"See. I knew you weren't all right."

"But you're all right I suppose. I mean we just killed a guy."

"You want me to get all touchy-feely and say I regretted it?"

"Fuck yourself."

"He was a piece of shit and one of these nights he was gonna kill a friend of ours. Maybe he wouldn't even have done it on purpose. He'd just be beating on her some night and he'd do it by accident. But one way or another he'd kill her. And we'd have to admit to ourselves that we could've stopped it."

I walked away from the edge of the porch and started down the stairs.

"You doin' better now?" Ralph called.

"Yeah; yeah, I guess I am."

"Clint Eastwood, I tell ya. Clint Eastwood every time."

Turned out Neely wasn't dead after all. We had to stand there for quite awhile watching him bleed to death.

I was visiting my oldest son in Phoenix (way too hot for me) when I learned Ralph had died. I'd logged on to the hometown paper website and there was his name at the top of the obituaries. The photo must have been taken when he was in his early twenties. I barely recognized him. Heart attack. He'd been dead for a day before a neighbor of his got suspicious and asked the apartment house manager to open Ralph's door. I thought of what he'd said about flying solo that time.

Ralph had experienced the ultimate in flying solo, death. I hoped that whatever he thought was on the other side came true for him. I still hadn't figured out what I hoped would be there. If anything would be there at all.

The doc told me they'd be putting me back on chemo again. The lab reports were getting bad fast. The nurses in chemo commiserated with me as if Ralph had been a family member. There'd been a number of things I hadn't liked about him and he hadn't liked about me. Those things never got resolved and maybe they didn't need to. Maybe flying solo was all we needed for a bond. One thing for sure. The chemo room hours seemed a lot longer with him gone. I even got sentimental once and put a Clint Eastwood DVD in the machine, film called *Tightrope*. Surprised myself by liking it more than not liking it.

I was sitting in my recliner one day when one of the newer nurses sat down and started talking in a very low voice. "There's this guy we each gave five hundred dollars to. You know, a down payment. He said he was setting up this group trip to the Grand Canyon. You know, through this group therapy thing I go to. Then we found out that he scams a lot of people this way. Groups, I mean. We called the Better Business Bureau and the police. But I guess he covers his tracks pretty well. Actually takes some of the groups on the trips. Five hundred is a lot of money if you're a single mother."

The chemo was taking its toll. But I figured I owed it to Ralph to help her out. And besides, I wanted to see how I did on my own.

---

So here I am tonight. I've followed him from his small house to his round of singles bars and finally to the apartment complex where the woman lives. The one he picked up in the last bar. He's got to come out sometime.

I've got the Louisville Slugger laid across my lap and the Cubs cap cinched in place. I won't put the shades on till I see him. No sense straining my eyes. Not at my age.

I miss Ralph. About now he'd be working himself up doing his best Clint Eastwood and trying to dazzle me with all his bad cop stories.

I'm pretty sure I can handle this but even if it works out all right, it's still flying solo. And let me tell you, flying solo can get to be pretty damned lonely.

# THE OUTHOUSE

*Ronald Kelly*

"COME ON, GUYS. THIS IS GONNA BE GREAT!"
Frank Bennett and Bubba Cole looked at one another, their faces like pale masks in the October moonlight. They had no idea why they had let Mike Stinson talk them into coming way out there on the south end of Green Creek. Maybe they had just gotten downright bored with the way that Halloween night had progressed: kicking back a few beers that Mike had liberated from the little fridge in his dad's den, then rolling the yards of the high school principal and egging a few windshields from the overpass of Interstate 24.

The three trudged up an embankment, pulling themselves along by fistfuls of kudzu and the twisted trunks of small saplings, until they reached the top. They rested for a moment, winded by the climb, which seemed unlikely since they were the quarterback, running back, and linebacker for the Bedloe County Bears, state champions for three seasons straight. They figured it was the alcohol more than anything else that was slowing them down and Mike had gotten a head start on them before he had even picked them up in his Chevy S-10 pickup around seven-thirty that night.

Their fearless leader flashed that handsome, smart-ass grin of his—the one that had gotten him in a dozen fights and laid by a dozen girls during his junior year—and pointed across the rural stream to the top of an adjacent ridge of trees and bramble. "There she is, boys."

Frank clung to a sapling to steady himself and peered across the narrow hollow to a narrow, wooden structure that stood perched on the opposite side. "It's an outhouse," he said, unimpressed.

"Hell, yeah!" Mike took the last long sip from a tall boy in his hand, then flung the can into the creek bed. "Tonight's crowning glory."

"Pushing some old outhouse into the creek is your idea of fun?" Bubba asked. His big moon-pie face frowned, puzzled.

"That's right."

Frank shook his head in disgust. "That's lame, man. Why would you get a kick out of doing that?"

"Because that's what country boys like us do," Mike told him. "It's, you know, a tradition. My daddy pushed over outhouses on Halloween and so did my granddaddy. And, as far as I know, this is the last one there is here in Bedloe County."

Bubba looked around. "Hey, ain't this Old Man Chamber's property?"

Mike nodded. "It sure is."

# THE OUTHOUSE

"Un uh," protested Frank. "You can just drive me home. I ain't messing with that old fart. Everybody knows since his wife ran off and left him, he's turned meaner than a rattler with a belly rash. Keeps that Remington 1100 loaded with double-aught buck and lead slugs, and he ain't shy about using it on trespassers, either."

"Quit being such a pussy," said Mike. "We'll push his crapper into the creek and be on our way before he can even hop out of bed and pull his britches on."

"I don't know, Mike..." Bubba grumbled, doubtfully.

"Oh, so you have my back on the gridiron, but you go chicken shit on me when it comes to this?" Mike brushed his blond hair out of his eyes and looked wounded. "That hurts me. Deeply."

Frank and Bubba looked at one another. They didn't much like Mike questioning their loyalty, on or off the football field.

"Okay, okay!" Frank finally said. "Let's get it over with and get outta here."

"Knew you boys would see it my way." With a triumphant grin, Mike led them down the slope of the embankment, across the creek, and up the opposite bank. By the time they made the steep grade, they were nearly out of breath.

The three stood and regarded the outhouse. It was about six and a half feet tall and five feet wide, constructed of weathered lumber and a roof of rusty corrugated tin. The hinged door had the traditional crescent moon carved in the upper panel. It was completely unremarkable, except for one thing. There was a heavy length of rusty logging chain wrapped four times around the circumference of the structure, secured by a big Yale padlock.

As they stood there, something inside moved.

"Damn!" Bubba jumped back a couple of steps. "Somebody's in there!"

Mike rolled his eyes. "Right… with all those chains wrapped around it? I know frigging Harry Houdini ain't in there, taking his nightly sit-down."

The big linebacker's eyes narrowed. "Who?"

"Never mind. Probably just a possum or a raccoon. Let's push it off into the creek and head out."

The three placed the palms of their hands against the eastern wall of the privy and gave it a shove. Nothing happened. It didn't budge. "Again," said Mike. They tried a second time. The boards creaked a little, but, still, it failed to move an inch.

"This old toilet is built like a brick shithouse," said Frank. "What'd Old Man Chambers do? Put a concrete foundation underneath it or something?"

"Bubba alone ought to be able to push this thing over," Mike said in irritation. He eyed Bubba. "Put your back into it, hoss. Just pretend it's Calhoun County's pretty-boy quarterback and tackle the hell out of it."

"Okay." Mike had known exactly which button to push; he knew Bubba hated Troy Andrews of the Calhoun Silver Tigers, who was an even bigger asshole than Mike, if that was humanly possible. Bubba put his beefy shoulder against the corner of the outhouse, dug into the mossy ground with his feet, and pushed with all his might, his giant face grown red with the strain.

# THE OUTHOUSE

Wood began to pop and crack as whatever secured the privy to the ground began to give way.

"Do it, man!" urged Mike, laughing. "Get 'er done!"

"Keep your voice down!" warned Frank. He looked nervously up the dark pathway that led in the direction of the Chambers farm. "The old man will hear you!"

"Let him!" snapped the half-drunk quarterback. "I'll kick his shriveled ass if he comes down here giving me shit!"

Mike and Frank watched as Bubba grunted and gave the outhouse a final shove. It tipped over slowly, then cart wheeled down the embankment, crashing loudly into the rocky bed of Green Creek. It hit with an explosion of splintered wood and mangled tin.

In spite of the danger of doing so, Mike Stinson unleashed a hearty rebel yell. "Hell yeah! Search and destroy! Bedloe County Bears—One…outhouse—Zero!"

Frank couldn't help but laugh. "You just ain't right, dude."

The moonlight revealed what the outdoor toilet had been perched upon. It was a broad, flat bed of smooth gray stone with a wide crack in the center. Curiously, Bubba walked over and peered inside. Usually, in an old outhouse, you could see something through the toilet seat; maybe a pile of lime with toilet paper and a few random turds scattered across it. But there seemed to be nothing beyond the fissure. Only pitch darkness.

"What do you see?" Frank asked him.

"Nothing." He found a stone lying nearby and chucked it through the hole. They waited to hear the echoing report of the rock hitting bottom, but there was nothing. No sound at all.

"That's weird as hell," said Bubba. The big fellow turned toward them, shrugging his massive shoulders. "Must be some kinda bottomless…"

It was at that moment that Mike Stinson and Frank Bennett noticed movement behind their friend…where the hole in the rock gapped just behind his feet. Then, suddenly, the thing was squeezing out of the jagged opening and looming over Bubba, making him look more like a three-year-old toddler than a 310 pound steroid and corn fed seventeen-year-old.

Bubba saw the shocked expressions on his buddies' faces. "What?" Then he turned around and screamed.

It looked sort of like a bat, except that it was pasty gray and hairless and two dozen times bigger than any he had ever laid eyes on. The thing's white, sightless eyes stared blankly at him until he began yelling. Then it latched its winged talons deeply into his shoulders, ripping past the vinyl of his letterman jacket and anchoring into the meat and bone underneath. Bubba tried to lurch backward, tried his best to get away, but his efforts were fruitless. He was in the creature's grasp and going nowhere.

Mike and Frank watched stunned as the bat's massive, fanged mouth clamped over the crown of Bubba's crewcut head and bit down. There was the crunch of bone and a curtain of blood coursed down their friend's horrified face. Then, with a violent shake of its gray-fleshed head, the bat-thing ripped Bubba Cole's head from the column of his neck bone.

# THE OUTHOUSE

"What the hell's going on down here?" someone demanded.

The two surviving high schoolers turned to find Old Man Chambers marching down the pathway, dressed in filthy long johns, his white hair flying like dandelion fluff around his head. He held a Remington semi-auto shotgun in his liver-spotted hands.

When he reached the little clearing where the outhouse had once stood, his face grew deathly pale. "Oh shit! What have you done, you damn fool kids?"

Mike didn't seem the least bit inebriated now. Funny how fast you can sober up when one of your best buds is decapitated by some freaking, giant bat-monster. "What... what the crap is that *thing?*"

The three stared at the gray creature. It grinned at them, rolling Bubba's head around inside its mouth like a jawbreaker, before finally swallowing it.

"I don't know exactly what it is, son," the old man told him truthfully. "All I know is that it was safely trapped where it was, before you pushed the cap off that crack in the rock and let it loose." He spat to the side and lifted the muzzle of his shotgun, pointing it toward the thing as it struggled to squeeze the rest of the way through the hole. "Dadburned thing killed my wife and drug her down into its cave, lair, wherever, while she was sitting on the pot taking a dump and reading *Better Homes & Gardens*. I chained up the outhouse to keep it locked inside. Told everybody that story about her leaving me because, frankly, I didn't think anyone would believe me otherwise."

The thing was almost free now. Its right foot was caught in a narrow corner of the crevice, which looked as though it was growing wider with each moment. The pale bat-creature shrieked shrilly, nearly bursting their ear drums with its unholy resonance. It spread its lanky arms, displaying a wingspan that was every inch of twenty feet across.

"You boys get outta here!" hollered Old Man Chambers. "I'll try to hold them off as long as I can. And head down the highway toward the lake…not toward town."

"But…but…" stammered Mike.

"No buts! Move your sorry asses!" The elderly man began to fire the shotgun, pumping alternate rounds of double-aught buckshot and deer slugs into the thing as it unleashed its foot and lurched forward.

The two boys didn't wait around to see if he had brought it down. They leapt off the top of the embankment, landing in the creek with a splash. They scrambled up the opposite slope and tore through the dark woods, listening to the piercing screech of the creature behind them. Then the boom of the twelve-gauge stopped and Old Man Chambers began to scream frantically.

*Oh shit!* Thought Mike as he ran through the brush and bramble as fast he as could. *Ohshitohshitohshitohshit!!*

A second later, Frank ran past him with a speed that had led the Bears to victory, game after game. It wasn't long before the running back was a good fifty feet ahead of him.

"Hold up, man!" Mike yelled. "Wait for me!"

"Screw you!" his friend replied and kept on booking.

Mike felt pain stitch his side and he struggled to keep up. He had suddenly realized that Old Man Chambers was no longer screaming, when something spun over his head

# THE OUTHOUSE

and landed a couple of yards ahead of Frank. It hit the ground with a wet thud and, in the moonlight, Mike saw exactly what it was. It was Old Man Chamber's right arm, severed at the elbow. It still clutched the Remington 1100 in its twitching hand.

Even in death, the old man's fingers reacted with fear and panic. His forefinger squeezed the trigger again and again, causing the shotgun to discharge. One blast sent a twelve-gauge slug slamming squarely into Frank's left leg, blowing it completely off at the kneecap. As Frank fell, another blast peppered his abdomen with double-aught buckshot. The pellets pierced the muscles of his belly and lodged deep within his guts.

The disembodied arm spun on the ground and, in the process, began to fire impotently into the darkness of the surrounding forest. Mike continued to run and leapt over his fallen friend without a second thought. He continued to run for the edge of the woods and Highway 70 just beyond.

"Come back here, Mike, you son of a bitch!" wailed Frank behind him. "Don't leave me here!"

The bat-thing screeched again, much closer than a moment ago.

"Screw you, Frank!" Mike called back and kept on running. He glanced over his shoulder once and saw his friend lying, crippled and gut shot, in the autumn leaves. That and something huge and hungry and as pale and gray as newly-poured concrete lurching through the trees at an alarming pace.

Mike sprinted a few yards further, then abruptly found himself out of the woods and sliding on the loose gravel of the shoulder of the road. He regained his balance and ran across the two-lane highway to where his pickup truck was parked. As he reached the vehicle and wrenched the door open, he heard Frank's blood-curdling screams begin to rise into the cool night air.

He slammed the door and was comforted to find the key still in the ignition, left there for a speedy escape following their midnight escapade. He cranked the truck's engine into life and stamped on the gas.

As he pulled onto the highway, Chambers' instructions echoed in his mind. *Head down the highway toward the lake...not toward town.*

"The hell with you, old man," Mike said. "I'm heading home!"

He heard Frank scream again, but strangely, his shrieks seemed to come from above rather than from behind. A moment later, warm blood began to rain upon the truck, splattering the windshield.

Mike turned on his wipers, but they only smeared gore across the glass, obscuring his vision. Then beyond the red haze, in the swath of the Chevy's headlights, he saw the thing land on the center line of the highway. Clutched in the claws of its feet was the armless, legless torso of Frank Bennett. The boy was still alive, still shrieking hysterically; the flesh was peeled away from his scalp and face, leaving a wide-eyed, screaming skull in their place.

He jammed the gas pedal to the floor and sent the big truck barreling into the bat-thing in the road. The grill hit the creature dead-center in its chest, pitching it over the roof of the cab, and into the long bed in the back. The truck lurched precariously, nearly flipping as it continued onward, crushing poor Frank beneath its tires. Mike fought

# THE OUTHOUSE

with the wheel and brought the truck under control before it could roll. He eased on the brake and glanced through the rear window. In the glow of his taillights, he could see the thing from the crack in the rock, struggling to lift itself from the bed of the truck. It looked battered and broken, but far from dead.

Frantically, Mike sped up, then slammed on his brakes sharply. The creature lost its balance and flipped over the tailgate, landing on its back on the blacktop of the highway. The quarterback stopped stone still in the center of the road, then shifted into reverse and backed up, building speed. He ran over the thing completely that time. With satisfaction, he could hear—could actually *feel*—the bat creature's bones and cartilage breaking and shattering beneath the weight of the pickup truck.

After the truck had cleared its obstruction, Mike stopped and, through the blood-streaked windshield, saw the pale-fleshed creature lying in the road, utterly motionless. The boy sighed in relief. He sent the truck forward again, steering past the thing, as well as the silent, bleeding hunk of torn meat and bone that was once his best friend.

As he drove past a sign that read WELCOME TO COLEMAN and headed down a steep slope toward his hometown, Mike Stinson wondered if a trip to the carwash would eradicate all traces of the night's bloody outcome and if he would be able to sneak into his bed without his father being aware of exactly what had transpired.

Behind him, in the distance, he thought he heard an ear-piercing shriek.

*Impossible,* he told himself. *The thing's dead. I saw it die!*

But, as he drove onward, toward the outskirts of Coleman, Old Man Chambers' words came back to haunt him once again.

*Head down the highway toward the lake...not toward town.*

*I'll try to hold them off as long as I can.*

Mike's blood ran cold.

*Them.*

As the screeching, both urgent and hungry, grew louder and louder, he looked in his rear view mirror... and saw the moon turn black as the hole beneath the outhouse gave birth to horrors once forgotten...but no longer contained.

# LOOKIE-LOO

*Steve Rasnic Tem*

J ACKSON HAD MOVED BACK TO MONROE COUNTY A YEAR after retirement, three years after the divorce. Without the divorce he probably would've worked until he dropped, making Sheila a pretty comfortable widow there in Ann Arbor. She hated Tennessee. How could anybody hate Tennessee?

Jackson stood behind a purple avalanche of Catawba rhododendron like some kind of peeper and watched as the three large men in their roomy homespun coveralls cleared a lot of rotted logs and tangled deadfall. He'd been following them as they worked odd jobs all over the Smokies: clearing trails, cutting firewood, moving furniture, putting up barns. Folks just told them what to do and they did it.

He didn't know yet what their story was, but he was pretty sure they had one. Since he'd moved back here he'd been taking notes on eccentrics: that fortune teller living on the old Poor Farm, that granny woman who cured pretty much everything, that fellow in Gatlinburg who could talk out of his belly. Someday he'd make a book out of these stories, *Strange Tales of the Smokies* or some such. He wouldn't be putting the locals down—it would just show how interesting folks around here could be. He'd finally have something to say about the world.

Jackson didn't know if he was a great writer or not, although he daydreamed about being known someday as the Henry David Thoreau of Tennessee, who understood living in these hills and appreciated the mysteries they surely contained. In *Walden* Thoreau said "The mass of men lead lives of quiet desperation." Around here people got desperate and didn't have anybody to tell it to. Oliver Wendell Holmes talked about people "that never sing, but die with all their music in them." That surely was these people. That surely was him.

He'd first seen the brothers two weeks ago shambling between the trunks in a dense stand of trees, like apes with their too-long arms, faces a dark shaggy blur, and in the shadows with those baggy coveralls they looked like a family of Big Foot, or Cave Yellers as they called them in Kentucky. And wouldn't it be a hoot to include those monsters in his book?

Those coveralls must have been uncomfortable, it being mid-July and steamy. But they worked as if their lives depended on it, picking berries and seeds out of the bushes and trees and dropping them into their sacks. Jackson could tell there was something wrong with these fellows—something physical or nervous or both. Every once in a while one of them would jerk his head back and forth in a

# LOOKIE-LOO

seizure-like motion, and he'd turn his head and open one eye wide as if trying to see something better. They all three looked agitated and impatient, but about what?

Then another fellow would be moving his shoulders funny, so they looked tremendously swollen, ready to burst. He would leap up on a log or a big stone, teetering, waiting to fall or jump again, until he'd calmed himself down, and then he just closed his eyes as if he were taking a nap in that awkward position.

It appeared that whoever'd made the coveralls had kept running out of cloth in one direction or other so different fabrics and colors had to be added on. These men had odd, swollen shapes, and the coveralls had been built around them. So they weren't pretty outfits, but they were tailored.

All three men resembled one another with the same kind of rough face, carved from flesh and bone by a sculptor who really wasn't all that talented, who didn't have a very sure hand. One was smaller than the others—Jackson named him "Junior." The biggest one looked like a "Bubba" to him, so that's what he called him. And the one that kept turning his head around and looking sideways, one eye a little bigger than the other, he called "Walleye."

There surely were strange things in Monroe County: maybe some version of Big Foot, and that Lost Sea attraction that was supposed to be the largest underground lake in North America, and the ghosts of all those displaced Cherokees, and the tales about big birds that walked away like men, and the mountain witches and the UFOs and maybe once or twice a hitchhiking Elvis had been seen out on Highway 411. But these fellows had real potential. There wasn't a thing normal about them.

So he followed them around from job to job, taking notes and not a few pictures, keeping his distance but still close enough to observe their habits, just waiting for them to slip up and betray their secrets.

That very morning he'd followed them to the rough shack where they lived. He parked his beat-up Datsun on an old logging road and used his binoculars to spy right through their open front door. At one point he saw an old woman's hideously-scarred naked back. She wore this silly hat loaded with feathers, as if she were getting ready to go out to some high-class society do, but she'd forgotten to put on her blouse. This afternoon, peeking at them from behind these big purple flowers like some kind of low-life voyeur, he thought there was something different about them, an increased nervousness maybe, as if they knew they were being watched. Every once in a while the smaller one, Junior, would jerk his head up and twist around, staring as if he'd heard something. Jackson stood perfectly still, wondering what excuse he could make if they caught him.

Walleye, whose mismatched eyes made him look surprised or suspicious, kept messing with the zipper on his coveralls and shrugging, adjusting their fit. The zipper came down a bit, and something dark and ragged sprang out before Walleye tucked it back in.

"What you doin' here?" the deep scratch of a voice asked behind him. Jackson turned around. Bubba stood there, and Jackson realized the binoculars and the distance had been flattering. The fellow was far uglier close up.

# LOOKIE-LOO

"Trespasser," came out with a spit, scraped up from inside the big man's chest.

Jackson made himself smaller, the way you were supposed to do if you ever ran into an angry bear. But it was hard to look away. It looked as if Bubba had tried to shave both his face and his scalp, and the hair had resisted, or he'd just been clumsy, because he had little nicks and scars everywhere, and the remaining stubble was too tough, each whisker too thick, like heavy-gauge wire, and there were all these protrusions that looked like tubing that had been severed at the surface of his skin, but the roots went deep into his face, as thick as straw, as if he'd been in an explosion, or the bad end of a hurricane had driven these broken stalks into his flesh.

"I got lost." Jackson couldn't think of anything else. "I was hiking."

"Hik-ing?" Bubba's mouth tried out the word as if he'd never heard of such a thing. "No pack?" The fellow stank badly. Jackson had a foul taste in his mouth from breathing the air between them. It wasn't much like any body odor he'd encountered before, a little like dirty feet mixed with kids' crayons, and maybe some greasy French fries in the blend. He'd smelled something like it before, around his daddy's old chicken coops and near the bird cages at the pet store.

"Didn't think I'd be out that long."

Bubba raised his heavily-gloved hand and pointed at the binoculars hanging from Jackson's neck. "Bird watchin', I reckon."

Jackson patted the binoculars. "Yeah. You got me there. Kind of a hobby, but I bet it seems goofy to you."

Bubba didn't look happy. He pulled his yellowish lips back to expose a large row of teeth that made a beak-like edge. "Some kind of lookie loo, ain't you?" he said, and the air whistled sharply through his teeth. That's what folks around there called fellows who stared too much. Peeping Toms. But the way Bubba said it, that whistly "lookie-loo," made it sound like some kind of rare and despised bird.

"I honestly wasn't trying to eavesdrop." Jackson knew immediately how lame that sounded, since it was exactly what he'd been trying to do. He felt seriously in trouble now. People down here were territorial; they'd had too much taken away from them.

"Don't worry none." The big man grabbed him by the arm. "Me and my brothers, we'll be giving you a ride."

Jackson was afraid to ask where they were taking him. They weren't headed back toward town, but farther up the mountain. The Smokies had some of the highest peaks in the Appalachians, but Jackson had never been one for heights. He was jammed between Junior in the passenger seat and Walleye behind the wheel. The smell was nearly overwhelming. Beyond what he had smelled before was this older, underlying stink like old and moldy cardboard.

Bubba was in the back of the pickup, standing in the bed, not holding on to anything. He had his arms outstretched as if flying, and the way the truck bounced when it hit some of the ruts, maybe some of the time he was.

The truck screeched to a stop so abruptly Bubba went flying over the hood, but still somehow landed on his feet. Nobody showed any concern. They were near the top of the mountain, at a small clearing bordered by tall trees, mostly white pines, and some of them a hundred fifty

# LOOKIE-LOO

feet high, maybe close to two hundred. Junior grabbed Jackson by the arm and dragged him into the center of the clearing. The brothers started chanting this high-pitched, loony singsong, "lookie-loo, lookie-loo, lookie-loo."

They stood around him, stretching, jumping up and down, looking increasingly excited about what was about to happen. They started making soft little scraping sounds way down in their throats, which after a few seconds became screeches and calls. One by one they shrugged out of their coveralls, great masses of oily black feathers popping out and spreading as their constrictive clothing slipped farther down their bodies. Finally the garments lay in rough pools beside them, and they stretched their muscles and fluttered, their immense black wings spreading until the shadows of them darkened much of the open ground between the trees.

Junior took off, whooping, climbing high and then swooping down, one edge of his wing tracing Jackson's left cheek and ripping it open. Walleye's turn was next. He kept low beneath the trees, his broad wings creating a wind that initially felt soothing against Jackson's overheated face, but then froze him in terror as the hard wings beat against the sides of his head and drove him onto the ground.

Finally Bubba dived in and lifted Jackson as if he weighed nothing, climbing parallel with the tallest tree to reach the top in a rapid ascent that stole Jackson's wind away. Breathless, Jackson viewed the mountain in a way he'd never seen before, the Ocoee Series of peaks spread out before him, ancient results of that collision of the great tectonic plates, and he was thinking what a perfect way that was to begin his book, which might now include the true story of the legendary Madisonville Tennessee bird men, when Bubba let him go.

—𝍵—

The boys' mother was looking down at Jackson when he woke up. This was the old woman he'd seen a few days ago, topless and with the scarred back. That feathered hat he'd thought she'd been wearing had actually been her head, covered with a thick layer of feathers that started around the eyes and flowed down around that jutting jaw and made a soft and luxurious, Renaissance-like collar around the neck.

The feathers had been partially removed from her torso, scarred and hacked at like the brothers' faces. Quills were thicker, tougher than hair, and would be a lot more troublesome to remove. You couldn't do it without a lot of scarring, a lot of pain. But she'd kept much of her plumage, so he supposed she'd stayed at home and let her boys forage for her. In her case the scarring was apparently decorative, or maybe tribal.

Forage. He'd been foraged. The bird watcher had the tables turned on him. Lookie-loo. She strutted around him, her head jerking back and forth. She made a soft and dry scraping noise deep down in her throat. She stank of birds and what birds ate.

He'd been in enormous amounts of pain. He'd passed out, and come back numb, then passed out from the pain again. Now he was riding a returning wave of pain—he could feel it rising from deep within him.

# LOOKIE-LOO

He told her, "The mass of men lead lives of quiet desperation. They never sing, but die with all their music still in them." He was delirious, but determined to have his say in the end. He had no idea if she understood him.

Her boys had joined her at the dinner table. He giggled, thinking it was a kind of Thanksgiving. They'd left their coveralls behind, and now preened in all their feathered glory.

Once he'd seen a bird eat a frog. You couldn't call it cruel because it was an animal. The bird had picked the frog up and dropped it several times, played with it to soften it up. The frog was still alive, but then the bird attacked it with its beak.

# DOLLIE

## Clive Barker

ELLIE WAS FIFTEEN THAT YEAR, AND IT WAS THE unhappiest year of her life. Her mother had died in the early spring, worn out by having too many babies, and loving them; by hard work, by the hopelessness of everything. The sky here was so big, and the dirt so dark, and though sometimes there were kind warm rains out of that sky, and sometimes the dirt gave up a little crop of potatoes, life was as hard for the family as life could be.

Towards the end, Ellie's mother had started to talk about how life had been back in Virginia, before they came out West. How fine the people were, and how gentle the air. Ellie didn't remember much of this. She'd been a tiny baby when they'd left. All she knew was Wisconsin: the bitter, bitter winters, the wasting summers. She knew how to write, a little; read, a little; but not enough to understand the family Bible, which was the only book in the house. There was nothing else to occupy her mind. Her only plaything was a wooden doll, which her father had made on her sixth birthday. Over the years she'd lost the crude features that her father had painted on her little head; she was just a naked shape. After her mother's death, her life became even harder for Ellie. She had to keep house in her mother's stead, cooking for her brothers and her two younger sisters and her father, doing her best to make what little food could be grown or hunted to feed six hungry mouths. She was neither happy nor sad most of the time. She had no expectation for her life.

One day, her father said: "That doll of yours. Get rid of it."

"Why Papa?"

"You're not a child anymore. Get rid of it."

She feared her father when he was cross, so she did as she was instructed. She told him she'd put the doll in the fire, but this was not the truth. She went down to the river, to a little strand of old oaks where she'd played as a child, and she hid Dollie in a hole between the roots.

The next year, there was a man from Boston called Jack Matthews, who asked to marry her. She didn't like him very much, but it was a chance to get away from the house, and maybe begin a better life.

She married Jack Matthews in the summer, and he took her back east. Barely a week passed before she began to see a side of him he'd hidden from her. He didn't want a wife, he wanted a servant, and when she didn't jump to it fast enough for him, he became violent. She wasn't a weeper; she took his abuse in silence, and only shed a tear when his back was turned. In bed, he was virtually useless, for which he also blamed her, finding further reason for violence. But what was she to do? There was nobody to

# DOLLIE

turn to for help. She had no money of her own, and she was very far from home. And even supposing she'd upped and left, to try and make her way back to Wisconsin: what awaited her there if she made it? More days of dirt and sky? Better, she thought, to endure her husband. Perhaps he'd mellow as the years went on. Perhaps she'd even learn to love him a little.

But life didn't get any better. They went from town to town, and he'd get a job for a while, she'd do some laundering, and there'd be a few weeks of calm. Then things, for one reason or another, would start to fall apart. He'd get in a fight and be fired, or they'd have to move on because he owed somebody money after a night of gambling. Sometimes she wanted to kill him. She even thought of ways to do it, while she laundered. A pillow over his face while he was in a drunken stupor; or poison in his coffee. Would God blame her so much if she ridded the world of Jack Matthews? Surely not. But the plans never came to anything. However much she hated him—and she hated him to her marrow—she couldn't bring herself to kill him.

The only pleasure in her life came from an unlikely source. She often laundered the bed-linen that came out of whore houses (which was the lowliest form of a lowly profession), and through her coming and going to these disreputable places, she got to know some of the women. Though she had neither the looks nor the confidence to do what they did, she had much in common with them, not least a deep contempt for the opposite sex. Many, like her, had seen life out in the wilderness, and had fled from it. And most would not have cared to return to the life they'd left. To be sure, whoring was no great pleasure to them, but even a modest bordello provided its little luxuries—clean linen, perfume soap, sometimes a fancy gown—which they would never have had out on the frontier.

She learned to laugh with these women: she learned to voice her rage at the stupidity of men. She learned a great deal else, besides, that she would have blushed to admit. She had never known, for instance, that often women pleasured themselves (and sometimes one another); nor that there were devices made for such pleasurings. Toys made of polished wood shaped like a man's sex, but more reliably hard. One of the women she met had quite a little collection of these things, including one carved from the tusk of an elephant, which she said was the best, because it was so silky smooth. One night, she offered to show Ellie how she used it to best effect, and Ellie sat and watched while the woman gave her what would turn out to be the most important lesson of her life.

Two years went by. The nomadic life continued for Ellie and Jack, a by now predictable pattern of arrival, hard labor, violence and quick departure. As her husband's state of mind slowly deteriorated, thanks to drink and innumerable beatings, his abuse of Ellie escalated. But—though the women she knew advised countless times to part from Jack before he killed her—Ellie couldn't bring herself to leave him. He was pathetic, yes; but he was all she had in the world. Then, one night, after Jack had been particularly brutal, she had a strange dream. She was back in Wisconsin, standing on the doorstep of the cabin, and she heard a voice calling to her. It was a sweet, familiar voice, but it was neither that of a man or

# DOLLIE

a woman. She went out looking for whoever it was who was calling her, and the journey led her down to the river. Now, as she walked beneath the ancient trees that drooped their summer boughs towards the water, she knew who was calling her. Her dream-self knelt down beneath the oldest of the oaks, and she dug between the roots. There in the dark earth was dollie. As her fingertips grazed the familiar form, she heard, somewhere close by, the sound of somebody gasping for breath. It was a horrid, desperate sound. She glanced back over her shoulder for a moment but she could see nothing, so she returned to the business of unearthing dollie. But the choking sound got louder and louder, she began to feel some force buffeting her.

"Let me alone!" she said.

The din just grew worse, the buffeting stronger. The dream began to recede. Dollie fell out of her fingers, back into the ground.

And suddenly she was awake, and the bed was shaking, and Jack was jerking around, with his hands to his throat. She got up out of bed. It was just about dawn. There was enough light to see his agony: the way his body thrashed, and his eyes started from their sockets in terror. There were flecks of spittle around his mouth, and a dark patch at his groin where he'd voided himself.

She did nothing. He seemed to see her there, watching him in this terrible state, but she wasn't sure. The seizure, or whatever it was, had such a grip on him that eventually it threw him off the bed, and he died there, on the floor before her, with the stink of his bowels and bladder rising from him.

She took virtually nothing with her. She just left, without saying a word to anyone. Who was she going to tell? And who would care anyway? Perhaps God had had some use for her husband: but if so, then He was the only one.

It took her seven weeks to get to Wisconsin, and almost every night she heard dollie's voice in her dreams. Had she not done so, she would not have gone.

When she got back she found the cabin deserted. There was still some furniture, but the few possessions the family had owned—a kettle, some pots and pans, a broom, and so on—had gone. She slept on the floor that night, and the next day went around the neighborhood to find out what had happened to everyone. They'd moved away to Oregon, she was told, about three months before. Nobody had an address of course, because the travelers hadn't known where they were going. She never saw any of them again; or even heard news of them.

Folks were kind to her. They supplied her with the bare essentials so that she could get settled back into the cabin, and that's what she did. A few people said she could come and live in town, but she didn't want that. She'd live alone, she said, and see how it suited her.

As it turned out, it suited her very well. She got herself a job at the feed store in town, and that made her enough money to fix up the cabin, and put food on the table.

For company she had dollie. She'd gone down to the river the day after she arrived, and her doll was there, where she'd hidden her years before. A little damp from being hidden in the earth, of course, but she dried out quite nicely. One night, sitting by the window watching

# DOLLIE

the sun go down, a queer little thought came into her head. The next day she bought a whittling knife in town and set about refashioning dollie so that her company might be more pleasurable. She didn't hurry; this was a job she wanted to do just right. Off came the arms and the legs; off came the ears, and all but a tiny nub of nose. The body she thinned out a little, but not too much. A sense of fullness was important, her friend the whore had instructed. She put some little furrows here and there, just to add some spice to the sensation. Then, sitting peacefully in a rocking chair (which had been her only concession to luxury) she hoisted up her skirts, and had a little party with dollie. It was perfectly grand.

She lived to be eighty-nine, and never had any other person, man or woman, under her roof for company, right to the end. Nor, she would have said, needed any.

# THE COLLECTED SHORT STORIES OF FREDDIE PROTHERO

Introduction by Torless Magnussen, Ph.D.

*Peter Straub*

THE PRESENT VOLUME PRESENTS IN CHRONOLOGICAL order every known short story written by Frederick "Freddie" Prothero. Of causes that must ever remain obscure, he died "flying solo," his expression for venturing out in search of solitude, in a field two blocks from his house in Prospect Fair, Connecticut. His death took place in January, 1988, nine months before his ninth birthday. It was a Sunday. At the hour of his death, approximately four o'clock of a bright, cold, snow-occluded day, the writer was wearing a hooded tan snowsuit he had in fact technically outgrown; a red woolen scarf festooned with "pills"; an imitation Aran knit sweater, navy blue with cables; a green-and-blue plaid shirt from Sam's; dark green corduroys with cuffs beginning to grow ragged; a shapeless white Jockey T-shirt also worn the day previous; Jockey briefs, once white, now stained lemon yellow across the Y-front; white tube socks; Tru-Value Velcro sneakers, so abraded as nearly to be threadbare; and black calf-high rubber boots with six metal buckles.

The inscription on the toaster-sized tombstone in Prospect Fair's spacious Gullikson & Son Cemetery reads *Frederick Michael Prothero, 1979-1988. A New Angel in Heaven.* In that small span of years, really in a mere three of those not-yet eight-and-a-half years, Freddie Prothero went from apprenticeship to mastery with unprecedented speed, in the process authoring ten of the most visionary short stories in the English language. It is my belief that this collection will now stand as a definitive monument to the unique merits—and difficulties!—presented by the only genuine prodigy in American literature.

That Prothero's fiction permits a multiplicity of interpretations supplies a portion, though scarcely all, of its interest to both the academic and the general reader. Beginning in 1984 with childish, nearly brutal simplicity and evolving toward the more polished (though still in fact unfinished) form of expression seen in the work of his later years, these stories were apparently presented to his mother, Varda Prothero, *nee´* Barthelmy. (*Baathy, baathy, momma sai.*)In any case, Momma Baathy Prothero preserved them (perhaps after the fact?) in individual manila files within in a snug, smoothly mortised and sanded cherrywood box.

# THE COLLECTED SHORT STORIES OF FREDDIE PROTHERO

As the above example demonstrates, the earliest Prothero, the stories written from his fifth to seventh years, displays the improvised variant spelling long encouraged by American primary schools. The reader will easily decipher the childish code, although I should perhaps explain that "bood gig" stands for "bad guy."

From first to last, the stories demonstrate the writer's awareness of the constant presence of a bood gig. A threatening, indeterminate figure, invested with all the terrifying power and malignity of the monster beneath a child's bed, haunts this fiction. Prothero's "monster" figure, however, is not content to confine itself to the underside of his bed. It roams the necessarily limited map of the writer's forays both within and outside of his house: that is, across his front yard; down Gerhardie Street, which runs past his house; through the supermarket he, stroller-bound, visits with his mother; and perhaps above all in the shadowy, clamorous city streets he is forced to traverse with his father on the few occasions when R(andolph) Sullivan "Sully" Prothero brought him along to the law office where he spent sixty hours a week in pursuit of the partnership attained in 1996, eight years after his son's death and two prior to his own unexplained disappearance. The commuter train from Prospect Fair to Penn Station was another location favored by the omniscient shadow-figure.

Though these occasions were in fact no more than an annual event (more specifically, on the Take Your Son to Work Days of 1985-86), they had a near-traumatic, no, let us face the facts and say traumatic, effect on Prothero. He pleaded, he wept, he screamed, he cowered gibbering in terror. One imagines the mingled disdain and distress of the fellow-passengers, the unsympathetic conductor. The journey through the streets to 54$^{th}$ and Madison was a horrifying trek, actually heroic on the boy's part.

A high-functioning alcoholic chronically unfaithful to his spouse, "Sully" was an absent, at best an indifferent father. In her role as mother, Varda, about whom one has learned so much in recent years, can be counted, alas, as no better. The Fair Haven pharmacists open to examinations of their records by a scholar of impeccable credentials have permitted us to document Varda's reliance upon the painkillers Vicodin, Percodan, and Percocet. Those seeking an explanation for her son's shabby, ill-fitting wardrobe need look no further. (One wishes almost to weep. His poor little snowsuit too tight for his growing body! And his autopsy, conducted in a completely up-to-date facility in Norwalk, CT, revealed that but for a single slice of bread lightly smeared with oleomargarine, that Prothero had eaten nothing at all that day. Imagine.)

In some quarters, the four stories of 1984, his fifth year, are not thought to belong in a collection of his work, being difficult to decode from their primitive spelling and level of language. Absent any narrative sense whatsoever, these very early works perhaps ought be considered poetry rather than prose. Prothero would not be the first author of significant fiction to begin by writing poems. The earliest works do, however, present the first form of this writer's themes and perhaps offer (multiple) suggestions of their emotional and intellectual significance.

Among the small number of we dedicated Protherians, considerable disagreement exists over the meaning and identification of the "Mannotmann",

# THE COLLECTED SHORT STORIES OF FREDDIE PROTHERO

sometimes "Monnuttmonn." "Man not man" is one likely decipherment of the term, "Mammoth man" another. In the first of these works "Te Styree Uboy F-R-E-D-D-I-E," or "The Story about Freddie," Prothero writes "Ay am nott F-R-E-D-D-I-E," and we are told that Freddie, a scaredy-cat, needs him precisely because Freddie is *not* "Monnutmann." "Can you hear me, everybody?" he asks: this is an important truth.

This precocious child is self-protectively separating from himself within the doubled protection of art, the only realm available to the sane mind in which such separation is possible. *Ol droo*, he tells us: it is all true.

It should go without saying, though unhappily it cannot, that the author's statement, in the more mature spelling and diction of his sixth year, that a man "came from the sky" does not refer to the appearance of an extraterrestrial. Some of my colleagues in Prothero studies strike one as nearly as juvenile as, though rather less savvy than, the doomed, hungry little genius who so commands all of us.

## 1984

### Te Styree Uboy F-R-E-D-D-I-E

Ay am nott F-r-e-d-d-i-e. F-R-E-D-D-I-E nott be mee Hah hah
F-R-E-D-D-I-E iss be nyce, tooo Cin yoo her mee, evvrrie F-r-e-d-d-i-e iss scarrdiecutt fradydiecutt, nott mee Hee neid mee.

# PETER STRAUB

Mannnuttmonn hah scir him hah hah
Bcayuzz Monnntmonn hee eezzz naytt
BOOOO
Ol droo


**Ta Sturree Ubot Monnnuttmonn**

Baathy baathy momma sai baathy mi nom mommnas sai
in gd dyz id wuzz Baaaathy
Monnoittmoon be lissen yz hee lizzen oh ho
Tnbur wz a boi nommed F-r-e-d–d-i-e sai Monnuttmon
he sai evvrwhy inn shaar teevee taybbull rug ayr


**F-r-e-d-d-i-e un Monnuttmin**

Monnuttmoon sai gud boi F-r-e-d-d-i-e god boi
En niht sai SKRREEEEAAAKKKK her wz da bood gig
SKREEEEAAAAKK mummay no heer onny F-r-e-d-d-i-e
Ta bood gig smylz smylz smilez hippi bood gig
SKKRREEEEEAAAAAKK att niht
Hi terz mi ert appurt id hertz my ert mi ert pur erzees
Bugg flyes in skie bugg waks on gras
Whi nutt F-r-e-d-d-i-e kann bee bugg
oho ha ha F-re-d-d-i-e pur boi pour boi


**Ta Struuyrie Abot Dadddi**

Wee go in trauyhn sai Dudddi wee wuk striits sai Duddi
noon ooh sai F-r-e-d-d-i-e
Bood gig lissen bood gig lisen an laff yu cribbabby cri al yu
went sai Mannuttmon
Daddi sai sit heir siitt doon sunn and te boi satt dunn
onb triyn wiff Mannnottmonn ryt bezyd hum te biu wuzz
escayrt att nite nooo hee sai nooo mummma nut trayn
Hah hah
Dyddi be nutt Mannuttmon F-r-e-d-d-i-e be nott
Mannuttmon Mummna be nott Mannuttmon hah no Cus
Mannotttmon izz mee Aruynt de Kernerr duywn de strittt
ever evverweaur
Deddi sai Wak Faysterr Wak Fayster Whatt ur yu affraitt
ovv WhATT
De kerner de strett F-r-e-d-d-i-e sai

**1985**

**The Cornoo**

The boy waz standing. He waz standing in the cornoo.
There waz a man who caym from the sky. The sky was al
blakk. I ate the starz sed the man around the cornoo. The
boy cloused his eyz. I ate the stars I ate the moon and the
sunn now I eat the wrld. And yu in it. He laft. Yu go playe
now he sed. If play yu can. Hah hah he laft. Freddie waked
until he ran. That waz suun. I waz in my cornoo and I saw
that, I saw him runn. Runn, Freddie. Runn, lettul boy.

### Wher iz F-R-E-D-D-I-E ??

He waz not in the bed. He was not in the kishen he was not in the living roome. The Mumma could not find littl Freddie. The man from the blakk sky came and tuke the boy to the ruume in the sky. The Mumma calld the Duddah and she sed are you takng the boy??? Giv him bakk, she sed. This iz my sunn she sed and the Duddah said cam down ar yu craazie?? Becus rembur this is my sunn to onnlee I doin havv him. I saw from the rome in the sky. I herd. They looked soo lidl. And small. And teenie tinee downn thur small as the bugs. Ar you F-R-E-D-D-I-E ?? ast the man of the ruume. No he sed. I waz nevrr him. Now I am the blakk sky and I waz alws the blakk sky.

### F-R-E-D-D-I-E Is Lahst

The Mumma the Duddah they sed Were Culd Hee Bee? It waz funnee. They cri they cri OUT hiz namm Freddie Freddie you are lahst. Cann you here us?? No and yes he sed you woodunt Now. The Onne who cumms for mee sum tymes is in Feeldss somme tymes in grasse or rode or cite farr awii. He sed Boi yuu ar nott Freeddie an Freddie iz nott yuu Hee sed Boi Mannuttman iuz whutt yuu cal mee Mannuttmonn is my namm. Mannuttmonn ius for-evv-err.

The boi went dun Gurrhurrdee Streeyt and lookt for his fayce. It waz thurr on the streyt al ruff. The boi mad it smuuf wuth hiz ohn hanns. Wenm hee treyd ut onn itt futt purfuct onn hiz fayce. Hiz fayce fiutt onn hiz fayce. It

waz wurm frum the sunn. Wurm Fayce is guud it is luyke Mumma Baathy and Duddah Jymm longg aggoo.
I luv yuur fayce Mumma sed your swite faycce thuer is onnye wann lyke itt in the wrld. Soo I cuuyd nott staye inn mye huis. Itt waz nutt my huis anny moire. It waz Leev Freddiue leeve boi for mee. Thenn hee the boi cam bayck and sed I went Nooweehre Noowehre thads wehre. Noo he sed I dudd nott go to the Citty no I did nutt go to the wood. I went to Noowehre thats wehre. It waz all tru. Aall tru it was sed the boi whooz fayce wuz neoo. He waz Mannuttmann insydde. And Minnuttmann sed Hah Hah Hah menny timnes. His laffter shook the door and it filld up the roome.


**1986**

**Not Long Leftt**

The boy lived in this our world and in a diffrent one too. He was a boy who walked Up the staiurs twice and Down the staiurs only once. The seccondd time he went down he was not him. Mannuttmann you calld me long ago and Mannuttman I shall be. The boy saw the frendly old enymee hyding in the doorwais and in the shaddowes of the deep gutter. When he took a step, so did Mannuttman his enymee his frend. The Mumma grabbed his hand and she said too loud Sunny Boy You are still only seven years old sometimes I swear you act like a teenager. Im sorry Mumma he saiud I will never be a teenager. Whats that I hear she said Dud you get that from your preshioys

Minutman? You dont know hisz name. When they got to the cornoo at the end of the block the boy smild and told to his Mumma I have not long left. You will see. I have not long left? she said. Where do you get this stuf? He smyled and that was his anser.

**What Happenz Wen You Look Upp**

Lessay you stan at the bottum of the staires. Lessay you look upp. A Voice tellks you Look Upp Look Upp. Are you happy are you braav? You must look all the waye to the top. *All* the waye. Freddie is rite there—rite there at the topp. But you dontt see Freddie. You dont't you cant't see the top you dont't see how it goes on and on the staiures you dont't see you cant. Then the man geus out syde and agen heers the Voice. Look up look up Sullee it is the tyme you must look upp. Freddies Daddie you are,,,, so look upp and see him. Are you goud are you nise are you stronng and braav are you standing on your fruhnt lahwn and leeniung bakk to look up hiuy in the skye? Can you see him? No. No you cant't. Beecuz Freddie is not there and Freddie is not there beecuz Mistr Nothing Nowehere Nobodie is there. He laft. Mistr Nothing Nowehere Nobodie laft out lowd. The man on his frunht lahwn is not happoy and he is not braav. No. And not Sytronng. Lessay that's truoe. Yes. Lessay it. And the Mistr Nothing Nowehere Nobody he is not there exseptt he is nevvr at the top of the staires. And he nevvr leeves he nevr lefft. Hah!

# THE COLLECTED SHORT STORIES OF FREDDIE PROTHERO

**The Boy and the Book**

Once there was a boy named Frank Pinncushun. That was a comicall naaym but Frank likked his naaym. He had a millyun frends at school and a thosand millyuun at home. At school his best frends were Charley Bruce Mike and Jonny. At home he was freends with Homer Momer Gomer Domer Jomer and Vomer. They never mayde fun of his naaym because it was goode like Barttelmee. Their favrote book was called THE MOUNTAIN OVER THE WALL: DOWN THE BIG RIVVER TREEMER-TRIMMER-TROUWNCE TO THE UNDERGROUND. It was a very long long book: and it was a goid storie. In the book there was a boy named Freddie. Al Frank's millyon frends wanted to be Freddie! He was their heero. Braav and strong. One day Frank Piunncushun went out to wlkk alone by himsellff. Farr he went: soo farr. Littel Frank walked out of his nayberhooid and wlked some more: he wllkd over streeits over britdches and throou canyhons. He was never affrayed. Then he cayme to the Great River Treemer-Trimmer-Trouynse and what dud he doo? Inn he jumped and divved strait down. At the bottom was a huug hall were he culd breeth and wassnt't eeven wett! The waalls were hygh redd curtuns and the seelingg ewas sooo farr awaye he culd not see it. Guldenn playtes and guldenn cupps and gulden chaines laie heept up on the flore. Heloh Heloh Freddie yeled. Helo helo helo. A doore opend. A tall man in a redd cloke and werring a crownne came in the bigg roome. He was the Kinge. The Kinge lookt anguree. Who are yoo and whi are yoo yallingg Helo Helo?? I am Frank Pinncushun he sed but I am Freddie to, and I was hear befor. And we will have a greit fyhht and I wil tryk you and ern all the guld. Lessay I tel you sumethyng sed the Kinge. Lessay you liussen. Ar we kleer?? Yes, kleer, sed Frank. The Kinge walked farwude and tutchd his chisst. The Kinge said I am not I and yoo ar not yoo. Do yuoo unnerrstan me? Yes said the boy I unnerstann. Then he tuuk his Nife and killt the Kinge and walkkt into the heeps of guld. I am not me he sed and luukt at his hanns. His hanns were bluudee and drippt over the guld. He lafft thatt boy he lafft so herd hius laffter wennt up to the seeling. Freddie he kuld see his laffter lyke smoke was hius laffter lyke a twyiste roop mayde of smuck but he kuld nott see the seelingg. He niver saw the seelingg. Not wunse.

# AFTERWORD

## Thomas F. Monteleone

Okay, so it's like a long time ago, and I am a single guy in the late Eighties and I am following my agent's advice by writing horror novels for what was then known as the "paperback original" market. All my contemporaries were doing the same thing—Charlie Grant, Alan Ryan, Karl Wagner, Rick Hautala, David Drake, Gary Brandner, Joe Lansdale, Chet Williamson, Rick McCammon, and Jack Ketchum are some of the guys who come to mind.

It was a heady time to be writing horror because we were all being towed along in Stephen King's wake like water skiers going a little too fast to realize how crazy the whole venture was. If you had an idea for a book that employed any one of The Ten Horror Novel Buzz-Words[1], or a cover with a skull or skeleton on it, your editor could

---

1   Black, Blood, Bone, Cold, Dark, Dead, Demon, Moon, Night, and Shadow.

pretty much guarantee you were going to sell around 100,000 copies.

That was great as long as you were writing at the novel-length. But what about all the people writing short fiction?

Good question.

Since this was not yet the Digital Age, there were still plenty of fiction magazines on the monthly newsstands. The genres of sci-fi, fantasy, mystery/crime, and even some western and romance titles enjoyed healthy readerships. But for those of us who wanted to write short stories that were unabashedly horror or dark fantasy, there were very few venues available. In fact, the only two I can remember back then were *The Horror Show* helmed by the late David Silva and *The Twilight Zone*.

But that changed when a guy named Richard Chizmar decided to enter the publishing arena with a publication called *Cemetery Dance*. Now, oddly enough, even though I've been charged with doing this Afterword with the assumption that it would be an informative as well as entertaining piece, I cannot remember the exact circumstances of how I became aware of this new entry into the horror genre.

I *do* know Rich contacted me to tell me about his plans for a subscription horror magazine, but I have no idea if it was by letter, phone, or some primitive form of email.[2] Why he picked me to share news of his venture I'm not sure—other than maybe we were both from Maryland, were both Terps fans, and both writers (and maybe he thought I was a cool guy). He mentioned that he wanted

---

2  I'm not even sure they had email back then—other than some weird stuff on Prodigy and GEnie (remember those?)

# AFTERWORD

to send me a copy of his first issue and hoped I would have time to send him my comments and opinions. Since I'd never been shy about commenting on anything, I said sure, send it along.

And so it came to pass that a manila envelope reached me with a postmark from a place called Riverdale, MD, which I knew was a centerfield throw from College Park. I opened it up and out slid a saddle-stitched mag with an 8 ½ x 11 trim size with a black and white cover that is mostly a pen-and-ink illustration of what appears to be a demon...or at least a guy with a long tongue and a very distressing skin condition. Checking the table of contents, the only name I recognized was Dave Silva, but twenty-five years later, let the record show that Richard somehow managed to publish fiction by Barry Hoffman, Ronald Kelly, Bentley Little, and Steve Tem (as well as Silva)—all guys who went on to have major careers in the genre.

In itself, an incredible accomplishment that bears witness to Rich's abilities as an editor and general go-getter.

Okay, now I have to admit, I was not blown away by the physical package of CD's premiere issue, and I think I told Rich in my notes to him later. And further, I let the thing lay around the house for a week or two—like that empty pizza box you *know* will eventually require your attention—before I finally picked it up and read it as I had promised I would.

That's when I was pleasantly surprised.

The stories for the most part were very well-written and did their best to avoid many of the hoariest of genre clichés.[3] There was also some poetry which was ambitious and skillful, and the general layout—while workman-like—was clean and very readable. In short, I was impressed. I held in my hands not only an immense amount of work for one person, but also the stuff of dreams.

Magazines like *Cemetery Dance* don't just pop out of some loamy soil like a wild onion or a zombie's hand. They only happen with mass quantities of talent, discipline, dedication, and a refusal to accept failure. When I think back that Rich was still in college when he created this magazine, I am doubly impressed. While most of his contemporaries were preparing for their graduate degrees in Budweiser, he was taking those first unsteady steps towards a full-blown publishing empire.

It's stories like this that support my belief that America is still a great country.

—◊—

Moving right along, I have another dumb admission: I can't remember when I actually met Rich in person. I know it wasn't too terribly long after that first issue of CD, but as to time and place, I got nothin'. What I *do* remember, when we were shaking hands for the first time, is that if I were casting a film about a young Roman named Cassius or maybe Nomar Garciaparra,[4] this guy Chizmar would have been at the top of my list. He had a rugged aspect,

---

[3] Okay, there were a couple of clunkers which shall go un-named to protect the guilty…I mean, I did say "for the most part," right?
[4] For you non-sports fans, he was a pretty good shortstop for the Red Sox.

# AFTERWORD

brimming over with serious determination, and he spoke in a soft voice that suggested quiet confidence rather than timidity.

I liked him from those earliest moments, and as the years clicked by, we became friends. We've played poker and golf and baseball together as well as talk books and writers and family. His magazine quickly became a standard in the horror industry and his color covers acquired a distinct "look" that became recognizable even if you were standing across the room and could not read the title. When I saw my first work published in *Cemetery Dance*, I was very proud of the credential, but it was nothing compared to the day Rich asked me if I would consider doing my M.A.F.I.A. column for CD.

My first thought was: *are you kidding—of course!* But I think I scraped up some decorum and simply accepted his offer.

I didn't tell him at the time, but I couldn't imagine a better place for my monthly screeds against the universe. The column had endured a checkered past, bouncing from one magazine to the next—as each one managed to crash against a rocky coastline of poor distribution and mismanagement before slipping beneath a cruel sea. I truly enjoyed doing the column, and wanted to find a stable home for it. I wanted a venue where I could establish a solid and long-suffering audience.

And so I did my first column for CD twenty years ago, and it's still going strong. I am listed on the masthead as a "contributing editor" although I don't really "edit" anything—even my column. I have always trusted Rich or his Editor-in-Chief to get my rants under syntactical

# THOMAS F. MONTELEONE

control. I often crow it's the longest running column in the history of the genre, but I have absolutely no evidence to back that up. In fact, I invite any of the bibliographer-fanatics among you to prove me either right or wrong so I can finally shuddupabouddit.

But enough about me—other than to say I'm extremely proud to have been a small part of what has become *the* classic horror magazine of our time. The book you hold in your hands is a celebration of twenty-five years in which countless new writers have been discovered, where new artists received a chance to be seen, and where established veterans were honored with special issues.

It's been a fantastic voyage, and if you've been along since 1988 or even anywhere along the way, you didn't really need to read my little homage. Of course, that wasn't going to stop me from having my say,

Rich, *amico mio*, you are the best.

Tom Monteleone<br>
Fallston, MD<br>
October, 2013

# ACKNOWLEDGEMENTS

With special thanks to Norman Prentiss, Robert Brouhard, Serenity Richards, Rick Lederman, Dan Reilly, and Hank Wagner for proofreading this spontaneous anthology.